THE INSIDERS

We Know what You're Thinking
And the Truth will be Told

Kathleen L. Hawkins

Windsor Westcott
❖ **P u b l i s h i n g** ❖
(817) 768-8332

ISBN-13: 978-0-9745452-2-6
ISBN-10: 097-4545228

The speech reversals throughout this book were
found on actual audio recordings. The story itself
is a work of fiction; any resemblance to actual
people—living or dead—is purely coincidental.

To hear examples of speech reversals
go to www.backwardmessages.com or
www.reversespeech.com and click on "Examples"

The face in the mist on the cover is used with permission of the
photographer, D. Sharon Pruitt, the original owner of the photo

1. Psychological thriller 2. Mind reading
3. Voice analysis 4. Reverse Speech
5. Speech reversals I. Title

Windsor Westcott
❖ **Publishing** ❖
(817) 768-8332

Rave Reviews for The Insiders

I loved the book!!! I read it in two days. Couldn't put it down! It was amazing. I can't wait for the next one. – Emily Plumer

~~~

I'm giving *The Insiders* five stars for sheer originality. And it gets better from there. To my knowledge there has never been anything quite like this story. Sure, murder mysteries are solved in psychological thrillers, but nothing has been written in which a mystery is solved by studying voice recordings of the suspects using a type of voice-analysis technology called "Reverse Speech." This is a fascinating, sometimes unsettling story that blurs the line between fiction and reality (the author makes up the story, but uses actual findings on audio recordings of real suspects). Read this book. – Lynn Dahlgren

~~~

What a wonderful "read"! I completely enjoyed *The Insiders*, and will recommend and share it with my two daughters (14 and 15 years old). The suspense was page by page, and the character development complex, but believable. The last chapter left me wishing for a sequel, and even better, the last pages seem to indicate a sequel will be forthcoming! Hope I can "pre-order" on Amazon, when that time comes. Kathleen Hawkins, don't let your readers (of all ages) down! – Mark Douglas

~~~

I really enjoyed this book. I hope there's a sequel. – Elizabeth McAdoo

~~~

This is a genre I don't usually read, but I thought the premise was interesting. A group of teens explore a phenomenon known as Reverse Speech. When a recorded voice is played in reverse, sometimes sounds are heard that resemble words spoken in "forward" speech. The group, calling itself The Insiders, believes these are hidden messages that express the speaker's true thoughts, sort of like how a polygraph detects when a person is lying. When two girls go missing, The Insiders decide to help the ongoing investigation by listening to recorded conversations and employing Reverse Speech to determine the truth. But not everyone wants the truth to come out, and soon The Insiders find themselves in danger. *The Insiders* is a suspenseful and interesting read. – Candace Williams

~~~

This book tells the story of a group of teen-agers who discover Reverse Speech. They use it to solve a murder, which lands them in some very real trouble. It has good character development and uses metaphors well. It has a dark tone, but truth prevails.

I look forward to a sequel to *The Insiders* and to further developments in Reverse Speech. It deserves to go public. Of course, just as in the story, certain forces do not want the public knowing about such a powerful truth detection tool. I believe that ultimately the truth will come out. It always does. – Austin Seraphin

~~~

Purchased as a summer/beach read while on vacation. I was really intrigued by the speech-reversal technique, which adds a unique and interesting concept for a book. I loved it. – E. Harryvan

Meet The Insiders

As unlikely a group of teenagers as you could find ....

Luke Nelson, 17, a high school senior, comes from a wealthy family, is tall, handsome, blond, and popular at school; life has always been easy for him—until now

Arianna Ladanian (Ari), 16, immigrated from Iran with her parents to escape religious persecution, doesn't trust easily, is trying to forget terrifying memories of Iran where her safety depended on keeping her thoughts to herself only to face more danger in America

Elaina Ramon, 15, the youngest of the group, works on the family ranch, is bright, likable, and funny, but anxious, her favorite thing to say to calm her nerves is: "Deep breath, no pressure"

Jessica Algren, 17, the oldest of the group, is headed for college in the fall, is beautiful, tall, reclusive, a vegetarian

Jonathan Rabinowitz (Jon), 17, will be a high school senior in the fall, loves NASCAR races and astrophotography

Kim Song, 16, holds a Black Belt in Karate, is health conscious, vegetarian, and the most confident of the group until the accident

Todd Draper, 16, cautious, guarded, and keeping a secret, but the mind-reading machine reveals it

Shanika Sabair (Nika), 16, outspoken, feisty, a talented soloist in her church choir, wears colorful African clothes, tries to be the moral compass of the group, but finds her religious beliefs challenged

.... united in an extraordinary adventure, the discovery of a "mind-reading" machine. The voice-analysis procedure, which reveals people's hidden thoughts in actual words leads them deep into the terrifying underworld of a killer's psyche. They'll be hunted for their discovery and soon running for their lives—and for their sanity.

iii.

CONTENTS

Speech reversals below are in bold print

Prologue

Night. The bright, full moon casts ghostly light across dark hills, a narrow river curves through pastures, a deserted two-lane road divides meadows and ranchlands; on the horizon train tracks stitch a long, silver scar.

A breeze ruffles the dark branches of scrub oaks and Whippoorwills call to each other followed by the brittle, metallic chirp of crickets. Bullfrogs, low voices reverberating in stock ponds, petition for mates and cattle doze under the trees. A coyote stirs the night with several high, short yips and then a long, drawn out howl—claiming its territory—and frightened goats press together for protection in a shadowy field.

The distinctive rumble of a Harley Davidson motorcycle interrupts the night as it pulls off the country road and up a long, winding driveway. Two teens get off the bike and remove their helmets. Luke—tall, blond, wearing tight jeans, t-shirt, leather jacket, and cowboy boots—turns off the engine, and walks the bike to the top of a rise overlooking a field behind an empty two-story house with raw, unfinished wood, sagging porch, and missing glass in the windows.

Ari follows closely. She's pretty with dark, shoulder-length hair, deep brown eyes, clear olive skin, and wearing jeans and a loose, long-sleeve shirt with buttons down the front.

Pickup trucks are parked throughout the field below, a couple four-wheelers do donuts in the dirt; the air is laden with dust. Men call to each other, carry folding chairs, coolers, and portable pens, which they assemble. Women visit in muted tones, children play tag. Dogs bark and whine. Bonfires are lit, lanterns hung in trees.

Luke eyes the scene suspiciously and rolls the bike off the driveway into the bushes. Headlights turn off the country road onto the driveway. He tells Ari urgently, "Get back!" and pulls her farther into the shadows. They crouch down, clutch hands. A pickup truck with two men in the front seat, a gun rack in the back window—and an animal crate holding a large, barking dog in the bed of the truck—bounces past them as the driver navigates the ruts in the driveway and drives down the hill onto the large field behind the house.

"What's going on?" Ari whispers.

"I'm not sure, but I think that was a pit bull in the crate. This might be a dogfight."

"I've heard about those. They fight dogs to the death and bet on who'll win. Why don't the dogs just run away?"

"They're trained to be vicious, given drugs to kill the pain, executed if they don't fight. A guy with a good dog can win as much as $5,000 a night."

Ari grimaces. "There must be 150 people. Look at the travel trailers and children."

"Yeah, 'good' family fun. Except dogfighting is a felony, and there might be additional charges for bringing kids. Those guys could go to jail for a long time."

Ari muses, "There are stories about this place: baying hounds, flickering lights in the woods, tales told by vagrants and drunks, derelicts not to be believed. Hey, look, the men over by the corner of the house, are they buying something from someone, tickets?"

"No, I don't think so; maybe drugs," then sarcastically, "This just keeps getting better and better."

"Let's call the police." She straightens up, visible in the moonlight; he grabs her arm, pulls her back down, "Stay down! These guys are real ugly. We'll be in *big* trouble if they see us. We're witnesses. They'd waste us in a second and not think twice about it; and no one knows we're here, no one would know where to look for us."

"That's it, let's go."

"If I start the Harley it'll draw attention to us."

"Then roll it back out to the road."

Luke shakes his head no. "There could be more people coming.

2

They'd see us leaving and wonder who we are."

A snarl erupts from a pen as two pit bulls are set on each other. Both animals are equal in size, muscle, and bone. Neither runs nor cowers. They slash at each other with glistening, foaming fangs. Fur bristles, eyes glow with an unearthly light. Around and around they go, stand on hind legs, brace against each other, rip and tear. Men circle the pen and cheer their favorite.

"This is making me sick!" Ari hisses and twists out of Luke's grasp, but he can't take his eyes off the grisly scene.

A menacing, moist growl comes from out of the darkness near them. Ari's stomach turns to ice and her ears buzz. She and Luke rise slowly, turn, squint to try to make out two figures in the dark—about 10 yards away—one holding a bullmastiff, a large, solidly built dog with powerful jaws and an under bite, straining against a thick leather strap.

"We saw you there in the shadows," the man without the dog taunts, "and I don't recall you being invited to the party."

The dog drools and strains forward against the strap.

The first man gives a slight, curt nod to the man with the dog; had Luke not been looking right at him, he wouldn't have noticed. He would have thought that the dog simply broke away from its handler rather than released. The man's hand goes slack on the strap; the dog plunges forward in a blaze of slashing fangs, glowing eyes, spittle, and rage. Ari shrieks, Luke grabs her arm, yanks her nearly off her feet—no time to start the Harley—half drags her up the gravel driveway toward the deserted country road. One of the men takes out his cellphone, speaks urgently to someone, "Get up here *now*! We got a couple of kids."

Blinding lights pierce the darkness ahead. Luke and Ari race toward the high beams. The light blinds the dog temporarily; it sniffs the air with its short muzzle and tracks them by scent. It hurls itself into Ari, knocks her off balance against Luke, her feet slip on the crunchy gravel, she screams and goes down on one knee, the dog's teeth tear into the loose material of her shirt; flecks of slobber spray her. It lunges again, Luke kicks at it and it attacks his boot. Ari's dark eyes glaze over, her breathing shallow, harsh and rough, too terrified now to even scream.

The back door of the car swings open; Luke shoves Ari into the dark back seat, the dog grips his boot. The car speeds away, the back door bouncing, still open. The dog lets go, drops behind, and howls in protest as its prey escapes. Men from the yard below scramble for their trucks and guns, fire a couple shots into the air. The headlights of half-a-dozen vehicles blink on and come streaming up the hill after them.

~~~

Ari gasps, lungs burning. Her vision clears and she sees Nika driving—wearing a colorful African-print shirt, her dark hair gathered into a bun at the nape of her neck—and next to her, Todd, pale and shaken, looking back, horrified to see the men in trucks gaining on them.

"Oh *nooo*, fire ants," Ari wails, and rubs her arms vigorously, "they must have been in the weeds, they're stinging me, *ow ow ow*, they're everywhere, they're all over me!"

Luke asks frantically, "Are you allergic?"

"I don't know, *owww*." She fumbles with her shirt, "They're in my clothes, get them off me, *get them off*!" She's crying miserably, her breath coming in gulps, he hesitates, and then tears open her shirt; buttons pop all over the backseat. He stares at her lacy bra, white against her olive skin, so beautiful.

"Would you two just get a room," Todd quips.

"She could go into shock, she could stop breathing if she's allergic!" He rubs her arms looking for ants, picks them off her quickly, one by one, pinches them between his thumb and forefinger, "I think I'm getting them, how's that, any better?"

She nods, yes, a little; her breathing slowly returns to normal and, mortified—no one has *ever* seen her like this—twists away from him, pulls the front of her shirt together, and buttons the one remaining button.

4

"Did the dog get you?" he asks and touches her torn sleeve. She flinches; he frowns, puzzled by her over-the-top reaction. Maybe it was cultural. She was from Iran where women are known for their modesty. "I'm sorry, I didn't mean to—"

Nika growls, "Stop talking, we're gonna freakin' die!" She clutches the vibrating steering wheel as though to choke it, "I need to concentrate." The car flies down the deserted country roads—65 miles an hour, 70—a white car, a perfect target in the dark. How fast can she drive and still keep it on the narrow road, 75 miles an hour? Distant lights shine from the windows of ranch houses scattered throughout the hills—too far to reach—80 miles an hour? The high beams press into the night, tires hum; white lines on the sides of the road guide them tightly around curves, across a narrow bridge, and up and down dark, rolling hills.

There's something at the side of the road, glowing eyes, an animal; a large coyote arcs into the headlights, they scream, Nika swerves, they brace for the thud—nothing.

"I thought for sure we'd hit it," Todd gasps.

"Maybe it was a specter, a bad omen predicting we're all going to die," Ari states.

"Does anyone have their phone?" Luke asks, voice shaking, "Mine's back with my bike."

Todd fumbles for his, but the lurching car sends it flying out of his hands and under his seat.

POP, POP, KA-ZZZING!

The back window shatters, Nika screams, "Son of a bitch!" the bullet whizzes by her ear and exits the front window, the car swerves again, she steadies it.

"Oh shit," Todd exclaims, amazed, "they're trying to kill us."

"Go to the police station in Dalton," Luke shouts.

DING, DING, DING

Red lights flash ahead. "Ah crap, a train," Nika says.

The crossing gate begins to lower. "We're dead," Ari states, her voice dull, resigned. Todd curls up to make himself as small a target as possible.

"We've got to get to the other side of the tracks or we'll be trapped," Nika yells above the deafening noise, and then to herself, "We're almost out of gas."

The train speeds closer, its bright, single eye piercing the darkness, seeking them out. It's as huge as an ocean liner bearing down on a rowboat. Death towers over them, Nika speeds toward it desperate to cross the tracks before the men with guns catch up.

~~~

John Paul, senior engineer for the Union Pacific railroad, sits in the cab of the 60-ton engine and sees the car speed toward the crossing. Who the hell is that? Trying to beat a train? *STUPID*! Try to save two minutes and get killed."

He calls 911 to report the pending disaster and then engages the dynamic braking system to reverse the electric motors on the wheels, applies metal-to-metal backup brakes, and activates the sander, which spews sand under the wheels to increase traction.

This isn't the first time someone played chicken with his train. He saw it dozens of times and it happened to other engineers, too, who weren't as lucky as he's been so far. The worst that happened to him was the time a large dog—its coat bluish-gray in the moonlight—tried to outrun the train. Get off the tracks, John Paul muttered through clenched teeth; just jump *off* the tracks and you'll be okay. But it kept running down the tracks ahead of the train. John Paul felt nauseated, but couldn't stop and couldn't go back.

Trains broadside pick-up trucks, clip school buses, waste families in cars, and kill drunk teens on prom night. My time was bound to come, when some jerk wad tries to cross before it's safe and I waste him. I've got a family and a good life; I don't want the deaths of stupid people on my conscience. I'm pulling 110 cars. It'll take a mile to stop at this speed.

The shriek of the whistle seems to be his own voice screaming his anger and anguish into the night, the brakes squeal, but the train speeds forward with a mind of its own.

~~~

"I can make it across, I know I can," Nika says.

Ari sighs, "I didn't leave Iran to die here in America."

"I'm sorry, I'm *so* sorry," Luke agonizes, "if I hadn't asked you guys to join the group this wouldn't be happening."

They grow quiet and Nika muses, "I feel calm all of a sudden. I'm not afraid to die, I know I'll see Jesus; I don't know where you all are going to end up."

"I feel like I'm floating," Ari says, feeling disconnected from her body.

The train's brakes shriek like a metallic banshee, the noise fills the car. Nika hunches over the steering wheel, "Oh Jesus, help us."

The car lurches toward the now-lowered gate .... slides on the gravel .... crashes head on into the gate ... a blizzard of splinters explodes in every direction .... the car bounces and rattles across the tracks .... the train clips the back fender .... it feels like they've gone airborne .... floating now .... floating .... silently in slow motion .... above the confusion .... the noise .... the night .... the terror.

1. "My wolf howls in the surf"

Six weeks earlier …

"I want to know why you're following me," Ari demanded as Luke crouched beside his Harley inspecting the front tire for road wear. She was furious with fear and so focused on getting answers from him that the voices of the kids coming out of the high school behind them seemed distant and muted.

He looked up. His compelling, blue-green eyes and good looks distracted her a moment from her anger, but she recovered and continued, "You've been stalking me for days, slinking around the corners of buildings, watching me."

"I might be a little secretive, but I don't stalk or slink," he smiled, amused. He stood up and raked a hand casually through his thick, dark blond hair.

He wore jeans, cowboy boots, and a white t-shirt; his leather jacket tossed across the seat of his bike. He was the quiet, confident type, which made him potentially dangerous. Ari didn't trust people who didn't say what they were thinking. It was too much like the government in Iran from which she and her family fled seven years ago. Soldiers watched innocent people—university students, businesspeople, teenagers, the elderly—"government opponents"—and before you knew it, the people they were watching disappeared, never to be heard from again, or were found tortured to death. A memory flares into her mind.

> "Welcome to the second grade," the teacher says pleasantly. She wears a dark, loose fitting, ankle-length robe and a hijab, a headscarf that covers her hair, forehead, and neck. She smiles at the six girls in the small classroom, "Before we start, do we have any Bahá'í's here?"

Ari raises her hand proudly.

"Girls, this student is a Bahá'í." Her voice hardens, "The Bahá'ís are a disgrace to Allah."

Ari's face flushes, prickles. The children's eyes bore into her; she can't look at them, instead stares at her clenched hands on the desk in front of her and inwardly cries for her mother, *Help me, mâmân come and get me, I want to go home.*

The teacher continues, "The Bahá'í's are morally corrupt; they let women worship in the same room as men, and—" She takes a deep breath for emphasis, and says on the exhale, "They don't have any clergy, there's no holy man in charge; individual members run their so called 'spiritual' gatherings. They're heretics and their religion is false."

Ari blinked in the bright parking lot, heart pounding. A gentle breeze swirled her dark hair about her face; she smoothed it back behind her ears. Luke stood puzzled before her. She cleared her throat and explained "In Iran kids followed me and bullied me for being a Bahá'í and the teacher encouraged it. I was scared all the time, but I won't be intimidated here. I refuse to be afraid."

He studied her sleeveless, lemon-color tank top tucked into low-waist brown shorts, her long, bare legs, sandals, toenails painted a delicate pink. He knew that Iran had a mandatory dress code for women; they had to cover their hair, necks, legs and arms in public, often wearing overcoats of sorts with long sleeves that come below the knees and under the overcoat, slacks or dark stockings. He smiled a little, pleased that it wasn't that way in America.

"Don't laugh at me."

"Oh, I wasn't. I was thinking how beautiful you are."

She glanced away, shyly, tugged at the small, black onyx heart—with raised golden symbols of her faith—on the chain around her neck; touching it gave her courage. She took a deep breath to steady herself and said evenly, "In Iran Bahá'ís are imprisoned, tortured, and killed."

"Bahá'í is your race?"

"No, I'm Persian. My religion is Bahá'í. We believe in the equality of men and women and respecting people of all races and religions."

"That sounds like a good idea."

"The Iranian government doesn't think so. Islam is the official religion. It's not safe for us there. My best friend—also a Bahá'í—disappeared with her family. They might have been murdered." She trembled.

"Or maybe they moved."

"Yes," she said doubtfully, "maybe they moved or came to America." She paused, drained by the memories and then bolstered by them. "Now I'm asking you, why are you following me?"

His eyes softened, just now understanding the intensity and seriousness of her reaction to him watching her.

And she saw something in his eyes she'd seen in boys' eyes before: interest. She was tall, slim, and dark, many would say "pretty." Boys were drawn to her, but guarded, maybe even intimidated. It made her feel powerful and in control and she liked it. But Luke was different. She was filled with fear and hope that he'd be brave enough to pursue her.

"I'm sorry if I scared you," he said. "I've been trying to get up the courage to ask you to join my group."

"Why would you want me to join you for anything?" she asked. "You have plenty of friends and you're on the school paper and in the drama club. I don't belong to anything."

He smiled. "You've been following my 'career'."

"The only thing we have in common is we're in the same English class."

She considered their differences. He was easy going and popular, a Texan by birth who came from inherited wealth, the grandson of a man who made a fortune in the early days of the oil business. She went to every school play he was in and sat in the dark auditorium feeling warm and feverish as she watched him on stage, but when the plays were over, she didn't go to the cast parties when the audience was invited; she went home. There'd be plenty of girls there competing for his attention and she wouldn't know what to say. He was confident; she was alternately apprehensive and bold. She made friends cautiously and guarded her thoughts and feelings.

"Well, I don't want to be in your group. In Iran our lives were in danger every day and coming to America cost us everything, our family business, our home, our friends. We left it all. I'm not taking any more risks." She spun around on her toe and stomped off.

"Wait, it won't be dangerous, I promise," he called after her. "We need you, I need you."

She turned back, "Why me?"

"I'm forming a research group. Nika's in the group."

"Nika from English class?"

"Yeah, and Kim Song."

She noted the diversity: Anglo-American, Luke .... Persian, her .... African-American, Nika .... and Kim, Asian-American. She was more curious now than suspicious. "Who else?"

"Todd Draper, Jon Rabinowitz, Jessica Algren."

"Jessica? She eats veggie burgers and keeps to herself. All those kids are pretty much loners and we don't even know each other. What do you want with us?"

"Just listen."

"Okay, okay," she relented and inched closer, cautious, yet curious.

"We need interpreters. A diverse group from different backgrounds might be to our advantage." His eyes darkened. "I found something that could change everything as we know it—and I mean everything." He motioned for her to sit on the curb with him, and said softly, "I want you in the group because **your wolf howls in the surf**."

11

She inhaled sharply and her hand flew to her throat. "I just got goose pimples." She extended her arm for him to see.

He was pleased by her reaction and elaborated. "You're tough and smart, a survivor; I like that. And you don't like Mr. Jones, our English teacher, do you?"

She lowered her eyes; if he knew personal things about her, he had a big advantage. Feeling confused and vulnerable, she crossed her arms tightly against her waist and resigned herself to being pulled further into his "plot," whatever it was. Her apprehensive eyes searched his for an explanation.

"How'd you know I don't like Mr. Jones?"

"You told me."

She shook her head. "I never said I didn't like him. In fact, this is the first time you and I have ever talked to each other."

"I recorded a conversation that you and Jones had in class about the meaning of a quote in the book we're reading."

She frowned. "So you recorded it and from *that* you gathered that I don't like him?"

His eyes swept the parking lot to make sure they weren't being watched, and then opened his saddlebag and extracted an iPhone. "After I recorded the discussion I played it in reverse using a special app." He took a deep breath. "Now it's a mind-reading machine."

2. "We share a face"

Ari was alarmed. On top of Luke being the sexiest guy at school, could he read her mind now, too? A chill swept through her as though the temperature outside dropped. "I don't want you to read my mind."

She felt as though she were floating alone on a raft on an immense psychic sea far from land, and a cool, strange mist had risen from the depths of uncharted waters. Tendrils of mist traveled up her body like fingers and she shook off the ghostly grasp. She rubbed her arms and, frightened, shivered in spite of the warm sun. How had he turned an iPhone into a mind-reading machine?

Luke interrupted her thoughts, "Remember how you disagreed with Mr. Jones about how to interpret a passage in a book we read and he wasn't open to your ideas? When I reversed the recording of you speaking, embedded in the backward gibberish were the forward words, **Jones, anger. My wolf howls in the surf.**"

She shifted uncomfortably. Her thoughts were private—or supposed to be. She could tell him that he was wrong, but the fact was, he knew what she was thinking.

He continued, "I assume the speech reversals **Jones** and **anger** mean that you don't like him. I don't know what your 'wolf howling in the surf' means, but it must make sense to you on some level because you got goose pimples. Do you want to hear it?"

"No!" she said sharply, embarrassed that he discovered her feelings so easily. The "wolf" reference puzzled her.

Luke lowered his voice. "Everyone has these inner voices, like some part of us—an unconscious part—speaks independently of us."

She whispered, "Like a stranger living inside us."

They looked up as a group of boys strolled past. Ari recognized one as the editor of the school newspaper, and another, the feature editor. Luke was a feature writer, too.

"Hey, Luke, you coming for pizza tonight?" one of the boys asked.

"Naw, I've got things to do."

The boy glanced at Ari and back at Luke with a slight smile. "Understood. Okay, later then."

Ari smiled to herself. Yes, Luke was busy. He was going to be with her.

Luke waited until his friends were out of hearing range, then turned back to Ari and explained, "All this mind-reading stuff started when I listened to music to see if there were hidden messages in songs."

"Backmasking. Some recording companies put words into songs for kids to have fun finding if they play the music backwards."

"Yeah," Luke said, "but there's something else going on. Here's a recording I made of my mom scolding my little sister Cathy." He pulled up an audio file. "Listen."

> Mom: Cathy Nelson, did you leave the rake lying in the grass?
>
> Cathy: *Noooo.*
>
> Mom: Someone could have stepped on it and the handle could have come up and smacked them right in the face.
>
> Cathy: Daddy did it!
>
> Mom: Dad's out of town.
>
> Cathy: Luke did it!
>
> Mom: He hasn't done any yard work lately. Were you just trying to help by raking?
>
> Cathy: Yeah.
>
> Mom: And you left the rake in the grass?
>
> Cathy: Yeah, I didn't know it was wrong.

"Now I'll play Cathy's last sentence again, and then reverse it. Tell me what you hear."

Cathy: Yeah, I didn't know it was wrong. **I knew**.

Ari gasped, "She said, **I knew**. She was speaking forward words in the middle of all the backward gibberish."

Luke nodded. "Mom told her a dozen times not to leave tools lying around; Cathy knows it's wrong, so she lied, but her unconscious mind told on her. This is like a lie detector, only better because we can hear what she's thinking." He thought for a moment, and then, "Actually it's more like a truth detector. When speech reversals contradict what's being said forward, the reversals seem to be the true statements."

"Are they the words themselves spoken backwards?"

"No. I think they're formed out of a speaker's stammers and pieces of the forward words."

Ari's eyes were large with disbelief. "This can't be true."

"But it is."

She looked at the iPhone suspiciously as though it might bite her. "We could learn a lot of secrets with this—if we really can hear the unconscious mind speaking in words and we know how to listen."

He sighed. "When people find out we know how to read minds, everyone's going to want a piece of us."

She nodded her agreement. "And I thought life in America was going to be simple."

"And another thing—" He stopped. Her dark eyes urged him to continue. "I think the messages are coming from somewhere deep in the mind. I've found some of the same speech reversals—like whirlwind, wolf, garden, and surf—on a bunch of people who don't have anything in common: kids, celebrities, politicians. That's why I want our group to be diverse, to see if we hear different speech reversals according to our backgrounds or if we all hear the same

15

ones. And if people use the same reversals, does that mean we all share a common unconscious language?"

He shrugged nonchalantly to try to downplay the enormity of what he was about to say. "It's almost like reversals are coming from a place where—" He stopped to see how she was taking it. She was, as the expression goes, hanging on his every word so he continued, "—coming from a place where we're all the same mind or spirit in spite of the differences—race, religion, and sex—that seem to divide us." He shivered. "I found one reversal that said **we share a face**. It's obvious we have different faces, so that particular reversal might mean that we share a common essence or soul."

She was fascinated and then frightened. "But some people think they're superior. The government in Iran kills people for having different religious beliefs. Even in America some people attack others who are different from them. How are they going to feel if they find out that we might all be the same spirit at the deepest level?"

"Maybe they'd be less judgmental."

"Or go crazy. If we tell them they're basically the same as the people they hate, that'd be like hating themselves, and then who knows what they'd do."

Her shirt stuck to her damp skin, her belt felt too tight, and her sandals felt like they were made for someone else and were too small. She wiggled her toes. She was uncomfortable in her own clothes and uncomfortable now in her life. Nothing fit any more. She ran her thumb thoughtfully over the smooth onyx heart in the hollow of her throat.

Luke asked, "So do you want to be part of the group?"

She heard an uneasy, detached voice—that must have been hers—answer, "I guess so." She felt numb and strange with apprehension.

"Good," he said cheerfully.

"I won't have to talk, will I? I don't want to be recorded."

"*Hmmm*, hiding something?"

"Isn't everyone?"

"You won't have to talk, but I think you'll want to; you'll find this so fascinating." He slipped the iPhone back into the canvas bag, put on his jacket, and climbed on the Harley. "I'm on my way to the first meeting. Hop on." He handed her a helmet. She hesitated. He said, "The others should be there by now."

She put on the helmet. "Where are we going?"

"To a haunted house outside town," he answered and started the engine.

3. Kenny

Kenny Lockhart collapses heavily onto the couch, scratches his potbelly through his dirty white, frayed t-shirt, and sets a plastic cup with a drink in it and a can of beer on the coffee table. He squints at the dimly lit living room. He's alone in the living room.

Is this room tilted? Or maybe tequila with beer-back chasers makes everything tilt a little. *Ack!* This place stinks, dust, dirty dishes, smelly carpet. This trailer is so old; crooked window frames, sagging walls, rotting floorboards. I'm lucky I don't break my neck on the uneven floor trying to get back to the bedroom.

Some inheritance, Ma, may you rest in peace, but dang, thanks a lot for this crappy trailer. You chased off my daddy, married a loser, had his kid Karen, he goes and dies in a hunting accident—shot with his own gun, stupid—and then you die of pneumonia with only $200 in the bank—not enough for one month's lot rent—I come back from Iraq with a case of the nerves, and get stuck with Karen.

So I get to pay off the trailer, pay the rent, pay utilities, feed Karen's sorry ass and pay her expenses, books, school supplies. Every time I try to throw her out, she begs me to let her stay. Well, get a job, Karen! But you're too young, aren't you? Oh *boohoo*. Babysit! But *nooo*, you gotta study. Well then, get good grades! And keep the effing trailer clean. You promised you would, but you don't.

He takes a swig of his drink, follows it with a gulp of beer, burps, picks up a piece of mail, scowls at it, tosses it back on the coffee table. Yeah, Mr. Bastoid, just keep asking for the lot rent; good luck getting it! You've got 24 other trailers, isn't that enough rent money? What do you use it for anyway? Not repairs. The park's an eyesore—collapsed fences, potholes, broken streetlights, no security. Any creep could walk in off the street and cause trouble.

He farts, smiles. That was a good one—robust and full-bodied.

It won't be long before the *la-di-dah* rich people in town complain that the trailer park lowers property values and force Bastoid to close it down; then me and Karen will be out on the street. There won't be any place left for us to live. All the new houses going up in the west end of town are all *la-di-dah* homes with tennis courts and swimming pools and golf courses; after a while there won't be any room for, how'd they put it, "lower income housing."

He rubs his temples hard, bites back a wicked anger building inside him, he's about to turn deadly as a Texas tornado.

And my freakin' boss lays me off from my construction job 'cause he's under investigation and might go bankrupt. So what if he pocketed the extra money that people paid for amenities, like gold-plated faucets the *la-di-dah* rich people can't live without, and gave them fake gold-colored faucets instead. Water's water whether it comes from a gold faucet or brass. It's wet! You drink it, or maybe rich folks got a different kind of thirst than the rest of us.

He tosses back another shot of tequila, hiccups.

Ahhh, liquid gold. Wish I could go dirt biking, work off some energy, but those damn tree huggers whined about noise and pollution and got the trails closed to ORVs.

He farts. *Hmmm*, that was squeaky, not as good as the last one.

Those tree huggers robbed me of the only pleasure I get. I want to kick their scrawny, little tree-hugging butts. I hope a bobcat eats them! *Gawd*, I feel lower than a snake's belly in a wheel rut.

He rummages through a heap of newspapers on the coffee table, discovers a dirty plate and fork in there, tosses them on the couch, continues his search, pulls out a joint, lights it, and inhales deeply, holds the smoke in his lungs, and expels it with a groan.

"Anyone home?" someone calls through the front screen door, startling Kenny, and then opens it and comes in without waiting for an answer; Sarah, Karen's friend; two years older than Karen and dressed to party, her thin lips painted red, big hair teased high, and short denim skirt drawing attention to her scrawny legs.

Kenny moans, "*Aw no*, Sarah, that's all I need is Karen's BFF, the 'nail technician.' Just say what you are: a manicurist!"

"Do you like my new boots, Kenny?" She puts her foot on the coffee table.

"*Ah, jeeze*, you're letting me see all your business with that short skirt."

"Just admire my boots. They're Chocolate Lizard."

"They're *brown*!"

"Karen's got a new pair, too. I got her a discount."

"A five-finger discount?"

"No, I didn't shoplift them. Don't judge others by your own standards. I flirted with the salesman and he dropped the 'two' off the $295 when he rang them up."

"Two-hundred-and-ninety-five dollars? You got someone to discount boots $200?"

"Yeah, it's a talent I have. Be sure to compliment Karen on her boots. They're so cool, they're Slouch boots."

"Perfect, 'cause she slouches around here all day long doing nothing."

"Slouch is a fashion style. You should get out more."

She looks down the hall. "Isn't she ready yet?"

"Who am I, her social director? She's been in the back for an hour doing who knows what. Karen, Sarah's here!"

Karen, dressed similar to Sarah in a short skirt, tight blouse, and big hair with highlights, skips down the hall and spins around to model her new boots. "*Ta dah*."

"Oh, I like 'em, they're so you," Sarah exclaims.

"They're so *yoooou*," Kenny mocks. "You're a slouch, Karen, and a mooch, too. Do they make mooch boots?"

The girls giggle, filling the room with the smell of cheap perfume and the high energy of young lives full of promise.

Kenny takes another drag on the joint. "*Jeeze*, you girls drive me crazy."

"It's a short trip," Karen quips.

"I'm gonna slap you silly, and that'll be a short trip. You two aren't worried about anything, are you?"

"Kenny, chill. I'm only your half sister so you only have to be half responsible for me."

She and Sarah giggle some more.

"I've got one nerve left and you're standing on it, Karen"

"Oh, *excuuuse* me." She steps to her left. "Am I off your last nerve now? Boy, I've seen beer bellies, but yours takes the cake, and keeps taking the cake, if you know what I mean."

"Watch it."

"I've heard of double chins, you have a double belly."

"Enough!" he glares. "You're a fine one to talk about how other people look. With your hair all ratted up like that and make-up thick as finger paint you look like a hooker."

"You should know, I guess. Who knows who you hang with."

He throws his beer can at her; she dodges it, curses under her breath, and then "Are you jealous because I have a social life, 'cause I'm happy?"

"Where are you tarts going tonight?"

"The Texas Tumbleweed, not that it's any of your business."

"I suppose it doesn't matter that you're underage, Karen, and shouldn't be in a bar."

She shrugs. "They let us in. We liven up the place. Come on, Sarah, let's go."

Kenny swipes in their direction, looses his balance, starts to roll off the couch, but catches himself on the edge of the coffee table.

A skinny guy opens the door and comes in wearing greasy overalls that say "Rusty's Wreck 'n' Repair" on the back.

Karen warns him, "Hey Rusty, watch Kenny, he's meaner than a snake today."

Rusty waves good-bye, "Have fun girls," and goes to the kitchen, looks through the cupboards. "Where are those cookies you had? Did you eat all them suckers? Is that a joint? Give me a toke."

Kenny holds out the joint for him.

"Where's the cookies?"

Kathleen L. Hawkins

"One thing at a time, Rusty."

"Can't chew gum and walk at the same time?"

"You got gum? I sure could use some gum. My mouth feels furry."

"It's a figure of speech, meaning can't you do two things at once like pass me a joint and answer a simple question? Focus, man, focus. I asked, where are the frickin' cookies?"

Kenny doesn't answer. He tips over sideways on the couch and passes out, mouth lolling open with a bit of spit dribbling out the corner, eyes rolled back in his head.

4. At the Haunted House

Ari hopped on the seat behind Luke and slipped her arms around his waist, thrilled to have an excuse to touch him and comforted to feel how strong and solid he was. She thought it'd be okay to rest her cheek against his broad shoulder—nothing indecent about that—and she closed her eyes, grateful to have him to hold onto now that her understanding of reality was slipping and she wasn't as sure of things as she had been before.

They passed the park, community pool, library, a bait-and-tackle shop, a trailer park, and the Get 'n' Go convenience store. Then they left the town behind and made their way along winding roads into the countryside, and finally turned into a gravel driveway that curved up ahead and disappeared into a stand of scrub oaks and mimosa trees.

He locked his bike next to several cars parked by the chain strung across the driveway.

"This is really remote out here," Ari noticed uncomfortably as they started up the winding driveway.

He caught her hand in his and gave it a squeeze, "You're safe; you're with me."

She frowned, was being safe that easy? How could anyone protect someone else against the unknown? But she was happy he was holding her hand, anyway. She lived as though she was always being chased by lions and scared of shadows. Luke gave her a quizzical look and she wondered if she thought that out loud.

"Nothing bad has ever happened to you, has it?" she asked.

"No, why should it?"

"Bad things shouldn't happen to people, but sometimes they do," she informed him, envying his casual sense of confidence. She hoped that some of his courage would rub off on her.

Gravel crunched under their feet, bees buzzed about

23

wildflowers, and insects chattered in the trees. Still holding hands they passed a bullet-riddled "For Sale" sign half-covered with clots of mud, turned a bend in the driveway and there it was: a huge two-story shell of a house in shambles with many of the windows missing or broken. Ari glanced at a window on the second floor—the only one with the glass still intact—and the shadow of a cloud crossed the pane giving her the impression that the house was conscious and blinked when it saw them.

Luke told her, "The people who were having this house built went bankrupt; it was never finished."

"Why'd you call it a 'haunted' house?"

"There are stories about wolves howling at night, lights flickering in the backyard, and eerie sounds coming from the house; probably just coyotes and barn owls."

"And the lights?"

"Maybe just kids with flashlights looking for a place to make out."

He let go of her hand, to her disappointment, and they climbed the rickety steps onto a warped front porch. He pushed open a creaking door and they stepped into a spacious entryway that smelled like clean wood, oak or pine. The windows were framed, but glass hadn't been put in; floor-to-ceiling windows about 16-feet high, Ari estimated. She glanced around the cavernous living room. There were recessed places in the walls for bookcases, an entertainment center, and two fireplaces.

Ari mumbled more to herself than to Luke, "There's something sad about being unfinished." She hated incompletion and demanded certainty in her life. She always finished what she started. The house was waiting for someone to finish it. It wanted counters, carpets, and fireplaces. It wanted someone to love it.

She screamed, "A snake!" and grabbed Luke's arm.

The snake, about five feet long, lay curled on the floor in the sunlight; startled by her scream it uncoiled and slipped away, leaving a wavy trail behind it in the dust. "That was a blue racer," Luke told her, "*not* venomous. It keeps the rats and mice away."

"A guard snake," Ari mused, and then added quickly, "I'm *not* afraid of snakes; I just don't like to be startled. Snakes shouldn't be inside a house."

"There are plenty of places around here for a snake to get in: missing window glass, uneven foundation. Okay, enough about snakes, people are waiting for us."

Dusty footprints led them down a long hallway. At the end of the hall Luke pushed open a door to one of the rooms.

Nika, wearing a short-sleeved white shirt under a bright orange-and-yellow African halter dress, stepped forward to welcome Ari with a hug, "We're so glad you came." Her thick, ebony hair had been braided and pulled back in a loose knot that accentuated her long neck and heart-shaped face. Behind her, Kim—wearing a Karate outfit with a black belt—sat on the floor and waved a greeting. Next to him, Todd and Jon—wearing painter's pants and khaki respectively—sat together against the wall and nodded a welcome. Todd was slim and artistic looking; his eyes flitted from person to person to size up the group and figure out people's agendas for being there.

Sitting in a corner by herself, Jessica was tall and willowy in a dark green, cotton sundress. Her eyes were heavy-lidded—like a cat dozing in the sun—her clear skin glowed, and her thick, strawberry-blonde hair hung loosely to the middle of her back.

"Thanks for coming, everyone," Luke said. "It was quite a challenge finding a time we could all get together with Nika's choir practice, Kim's Karate, Todd's track, Jon's chess club."

"What do you do for fun, Jessica?" Nika asked.

"I think," she answered.

"About what?"

"I think about thinking."

Nika wrinkled her nose.

"Philosophy," Jessica specified, "and I write poetry."

Luke sat down against the wall and took out his iPhone. The

group moved closer. "I already told you all about this mind-reading stuff, so let's get started," he said.

"Can we meet somewhere else next time?" Jessica asked. "This place creeps me out; it's tormented. There's an anguish here that makes my skin crawl."

Ari puzzled, what an odd thing to say, as if a house could feel tormented.

Nika agreed. "I don't like this place, either, it is creepy. And there's pigeon poop on the floor."

The kids laughed, which helped to relieve some of the tension that Ari was feeling about the uncertain adventure of reading people's minds.

"I thought it'd be fun to come here," Luke said, "before you pointed out the pigeon poop. I haven't been here in a while, but sure, we can meet somewhere else next time."

Ari wondered what he'd been doing here the last time and who was with him. Maybe he came to make out with someone. How depressing.

"Let's hear these speech reversals," Nika said.

Luke opened an audio file.

Ari smiled as she watched him. She loved his eagerness to share his discovery with them. His enthusiasm made him even more appealing.

He glanced up and winked at her. She felt a rush of warmth in response; her body had a mind of its own. She glanced away quickly, and then back again to return his wink with a smile, but he didn't notice; he was focused on the demonstration.

"Okay," he said, "I recorded this off the news. The speech reversals are on a guy who was captured after he shot some people. He's talking to the police. First you'll hear the forward speech, and then the reversal." He passed everyone a sheet of paper. "This is the transcript I typed up. The reversals are in bold print. Here we go." He tapped "play."

Murderer: "I was using the rifle." **The firing was easy**.

Murderer: "I'd half decided to go to my girlfriend's place, my ex-girlfriend's place, and hand myself in." **Murder. Shot the folks down**.

Murderer: "I heard the police car behind me so I turned in the alley here." **You know, I killed**.

Murderer (talking about the arrival of the police): "I thought they were outside behind the car doors." **So annoyed. Must have more fun**.

Police: "Do you have any regret over these people dying?"

Murderer: "Yep. I regret that it had to be civilians and I regret that I was captured rather than killed." **Hate. They're all the same, shot.**

Ari couldn't believe how easily they stepped into the middle of a murderer's mind like opening a door to his messy bedroom, private office, or dark, musty attic. And she felt a sinking feeling of dread. They were invisible here in a murderer's private domain and could snoop in his business to their hearts' content. They could learn anything about him if he gave them the key: his forward speech.

What would he do to them if he caught them here?

Jessica brightened with excitement, "I've always felt there's more to life than we know, a deeper meaning, something hidden. Maybe speech reversals can help us figure it out."

Ari nibbled her lower lip and thought that Jessica wouldn't know danger if it bit her.

Kim stretched out his legs on the floor in front of him and tucked his hands into his pockets. He was confident being in a haunted house about to embark on a weird project. He worked out regularly at the Karate studio his parents owned and he knew self-defense.

Todd, nervous and unsure of the group at first, now took some comfort in the fact that the others felt uneasy, too. Jon, looking studious in wire-rimmed glasses, rubbed his temples, feeling tense. He commented more to himself than to the others, "I should have just gone fishing like I planned to do today."

Ari looked to Luke for reassurance, reluctant to trespass on what was previously one of humanity's more valued possessions, the privacy of one's own thoughts. She didn't think they should be in this dangerous place, but was too fascinated to turn away. What if the murderer sensed them here in his private "room" and focused his grim agenda on them?

5. A Real Earful

"You look spooked," Luke told Ari.

She swallowed nervously. It wasn't helping that it was getting late in the day, the setting sun casting long shadows across the yard of the haunted house, and the light growing fainter on the wooden floor where they sat in the room at the far end of the hall. The last light through the trees dappled the floor about them, and a cool, fragrant breeze wafted through the room. She wondered if the ghosts were gathering. She didn't want to be there after dark listening to the thoughts of a killer.

The others looked at her, waiting for her reaction to the mind-reading machine.

"I'm not that spooked," she lied as nonchalantly as possible. She hated to be watched, to not know what people are thinking. She filled in their silences with worst-case scenarios. She wondered if they thought she was a coward and she wished she'd never joined their group. She suddenly felt very much an outsider in this small group of insiders. Jessica was excited about what they were doing, and Kim with his black belt was Mr. Confident. They were all braver than she was—or maybe she was just more realistic. Maybe she was wired to sense real danger.

Luke said quietly, "There's no way this murderer is going to know we're listening to him."

"He'll find out," Ari whispered, refusing to be convinced.

"I don't think he will," Luke said.

"But what if he does? What if he comes after us? He already shot a bunch of people and had fun doing it. He said so."

"We won't tell anyone what we're doing."

Todd ventured, "It might be hard to keep a mind-reading machine a secret," and then added quickly, "I mean, I can keep a secret, I'm very good at it, but sometimes secrets have a way of getting out."

"I want to hear speech reversals on us," Jon said. "Can you reverse what we say?"

"You bet," Luke said.

"You haven't been recording us, have you?" Ari exclaimed, alarmed.

"Not yet," Luke said, "not without your permission."

Nika frowned at Jon, "Are you sure you want us to hear your speech reversals? If this is for real, people are going to be able to look into the depths of your soul. It'll be like having people see you in your underwear."

Luke winced, "Well, probably not exactly like that."

The kids laughed uneasily.

"Okay, let's record a conversation, the more emotional the better," Luke said.

"Politics," Jon stated, and then, quickly, "oh no, not politics—religion! That's about as emotional as you can get here in the Bible Belt."

"Okay, religion," Luke said and tapped "record" on the iPhone. "What religions do we have here? I'm Methodist."

"Southern Baptist," Nika said, "Conservative."

"Me, too—Southern Baptist—but a Moderate," Todd stated.

"Jewish," Jon said.

"Buddhist," Kim said.

"Bahá'í," Ari said, and when they gave her a never-heard-of-it look, she added, "One of the world's fastest growing religions."

"I don't have a name for my faith," Jessica stated. "Just a walk in the woods can be a spiritual experience. I guess you could say I believe in the God of nature."

"The Jews are still waiting for the Messiah," Jon offered with a little smile, knowing what a touchy subject that would be.

Nika pounced, "Jesus was the Messiah," she exclaimed, irritated, "The Bible says he was."

"We think he was a great teacher, but not the Messiah," Jon

countered. "Besides, the Bible isn't my holy book."

"Baptists are waiting for His second coming," Todd interjected.

"What do Bahá'ís believe about Jesus?" Jon asked Ari.

He was surprised when she came up with yet another belief. "We believe there's one spokesperson every 1,000 years or more to deliver God's message. The spokespeople so far have been Zoroaster, Buddha, Krishna, Moses, Jesus, Mohammed, and most recently Bahá'u'lláh, a Persian messenger of God in the 1800s."

Nika groaned her disagreement. "So many? I think there was just one."

Todd asked in a small voice, "So how do we know what's true?"

"Maybe when we play this recording backwards we'll find out," Ari said.

"I don't want my speech reversals analyzed," Todd stated apprehensively.

"Wait, *shhhh*," Luke whispered, hitting "stop" on the recorder. "Did you hear that? Footsteps. Someone's in the hall."

The footsteps stopped. A door creaked opened, then closed; someone was looking in the rooms.

Ari thought weakly, ghosts, it's the ghosts; I just know it.

They sat silently, hardly breathing. This creepy reversal stuff— especially in a haunted house—was making them all jumpy.

Luke pressed the iPhone to his chest to guard it.

The door to the room right next door opened. And then closed.

Ari nibbled her bottom lip nervously.

The footsteps came closer. Closer. Right outside the room now.

The door opened and a girl with a big smile, round face, and dark eyes peeked in. Her shoulder-length, black hair bounced when she moved and her skin shone like polished bronze.

"That's Elaina," Nika exclaimed, "my friend."

They let out a collective sigh of relief.

"What's going on?" Elaina asked pleasantly and stepped into the room in jeans, t-shirt, and sandals. She looked younger than the rest of them, like a kid sister. Ari had seen her at school and thought she might be a freshman, which would make her about 15. What was she doing out here by herself? Maybe she drove. Some kids got "hardship" licenses so they could help out on their family farms and ranches.

"Nika's been acting secretive lately," Elaina said, "so I followed her to make sure she wasn't running with a bad crowd. May I join you?"

"Elaina's okay, I promise," Nika assured Luke. "I've known her since I was in the second grade and she was in kindergarten."

Elaina told them, "Mom asked Nika to walk me to school, and we've been friends ever since. Now I'm watching her—to make sure she doesn't get into any trouble." Luke was sitting in front of the group so she figured that he was in charge and approached him with an imploring look and a sense of humor. She clasped her hands together and begged, "Please, please, please let me stay. What are y'all doing? I won't tell anyone, I promise."

Nika warned, "You don't know what the group's about, you might not like it. It'd make you nervous," then to the group, "She has anxiety attacks."

"No pressure, Nika," Elaina beamed, "you're part of the group, so I'll be okay, and I hate to be left out of anything."

She was enthusiastic and bright—instantly likable. Luke relented. "Okay, welcome to the group. I recorded the conversation we just had and now I'll play it in reverse. You're about to get a real earful."

6. What Happened at the Rodeo

The bull explodes from the bucking chute. Four thousand pounds of pure rage pitches and lurches, sharp hooves plow up clods of dirt. On its back, a cowboy flops like a rag doll and the crowd goes wild.

Standing on the sidelines, Bobby Buller stoops to hug his seven-year old son. Justin wraps his arms around his daddy; how thin he is, thinner than a lot of the other cowboys on the circuit, but Bobby works out daily and is as tough and fit as any of them, and an even better rider.

"What do I always say before a ride, son? Say it how we practiced."

Justin grins, "If you're not living on the edge you're taking up too much space."

"That's my boy!"

He squeezes Justin's arm affectionately and heads toward the bucking chute. Justin follows. "When we go to rodeo school next week can I ride Mighty Bucky instead of Lil' Bit Bucky? I'm seven now."

Sometimes Justin and his dad go to the Trail Dust Rodeo School so Bobby can practice riding "Mighty Bucky," a mechanical bull and training simulator. Secured to the floor with a sturdy pole, Mighty Bucky spins and lurches from side to side in a random fashion to test a cowboy's riding skills and balance.

Until "Mighty Bucky Extreme" came out, "Mighty Bucky" was the biggest mechanical bull: four-feet high, four-feet long, and two-feet across. "Lil' Bit Bucky" was only three-feet high, three feet six-inches long, and two-feet across. Whenever Justin rode Lil' Bit Bucky his dad stood along side him and held his arm.

"Please, can I—"

"Son, cowboys don't whine," Bobby scolds.

"If I don't whine?"

"You've got to start out easy on the mechanical bulls and work up to the bigger ones."

"You could hold on to me, like you do when I'm on Lil' Bit, and put it on the slowest setting."

"This is not the time to talk about this. I need to focus on the ride today."

"But I want to—"

"Not now," Bobby says firmly, "I'm riding Twister and I've got to keep my focus. We'll talk about it later. Go get something to eat. Did your mom give you some money?"

Justin nods yes, holds up a ten-dollar bill that Sally gave him, and heads toward the food court. He has about 15 minutes to buy some ribs and get back to the bleachers to see his daddy ride the last bull of the day.

Sally, blonde hair pulled back in a long, silky ponytail and gossiping with friends at a craft booth, waves to him, "Hi sweetie! Get some lemonade; it's healthier than a soft drink."

She doesn't worry about her son wandering off at a rodeo because he's never alone. Justin and Sally follow his daddy from town to town along the circuit; and all the rodeo regulars—pickup riders, stock contractors, chute bosses, and people who own the booths—know the little boy and keep an eye on him.

A clown—wearing loose baggy pants, floppy shoes, red shirt, and a scraggly red-orange wig appears suddenly at Justin's side. "I'll walk him over, Sal."

"Dorky Dinky Do," Justin exclaims affectionately. Dorky leans close to him, and playfully bumps his forehead with his big, red nose, which reduces Justin to a fit of giggles.

"You laughing at me?" Dorky scolds.

Justin howls with laughter, "Yes, because you're a *clown!*"

Dorky sniffs, nose in the air, pretends to be insulted, "That's 'rodeo protection athlete' to you."

"Can I sit in the clown lounge after the rodeo?"

"Sure, if I don't pee or throw up in it."

The "clown lounge," or "bomb shelter," as it's sometimes called, is a heavy, 175-pound steel barrel lined with foam rubber. Dorky uses it during a rodeo after he distracts a bull from trying to gore a fallen rider and the bull turns on him. "I'm the only thing between the bull and a fallen rider and the clown lounge is the only thing between me and the bull." He laughs, "Being a rodeo protection athlete is a guaranteed hard day at the office."

Justin grins. Dorky gives the term "a barrel of laughs" new meaning; having Dorky as a friend is like having his own personal cartoon character come to life.

Justin has been going to rodeos all his life. His daddy told him how to care for livestock, shop for Western wear, eat three-alarm chili with peppers so fiery it'd make a grown man cry, and recite the rules for calf roping, bronco riding, barrel racing, and the most dangerous and exciting event of all: bull riding.

"What do you say to the namby-pamby animal-rights activists who accuse us of tightening the flank strap around a bull's tender parts to make him buck?" Bobby quizzed.

"The strap doesn't hurt the animal," Justin stated clearly, "it just gives him the incentive to buck hard and effectively." Justin didn't know what that meant, but he was a good memorizer and proud of it.

"That's right, son. It'd be stupid to hurt our animals. They're our livelihood. The bull doesn't like us sitting on him, that's all. And we tighten the strap a little around his flank and he squirms a little."

Justin wasn't so sure the flank strap didn't hurt the bulls—they sure did buck a lot—but he never questioned his dad out loud.

"Here's the food line," Dorky tells Justin. "I gotta go. Your dad's up next."

Justin shifts his weight impatiently from foot to foot in line. He wants ribs, his favorite: cooked to perfection over slow-burning mesquite, the outside of the meat wonderfully crusty, the inside tender and juicy, and topped with thick, tomato sauce laced with Worcestershire, Tabasco, and a hint of garlic, pepper, and lemon.

He steps up to the counter and Sam Bridges greets him with a crooked smile, "Howdy, young man, what'll it be today, ribs?" Justin always orders ribs. Sam moves slowly as he heaps a generous serving onto a thick paper plate and ladles sauce over it, then plops a big scoop of cold potato salad next to it and serves it up with a hunk of buttered Texas toast, a plastic fork, and a fistful of napkins. "Lemonade?" Sam asks, a twinkle in his eyes, one of which peeks out from under a drooping lid, and Justin nods.

"I hear your dad's riding Twister today."

"The meanest bull on the circuit," Justin brags, proud that his daddy is taking on the toughest bull there is.

"The meanest after they retired Twister's daddy, Bodacious," Sam says, his voice trailing off into a memory. "Bo was my undoing," he says softly. "He did something no bull ever did before or since: he'd throw back his head smack into the face of a rider and pulverize it. Broke both my cheekbones, blackened my eyes, tore open my lip—see the scar—and crushed all the nerves on the right side of my face." He rubs his drooping eyelid. "*Yep*, Bo was a worthy adversary. I sure admired him and the way he bucked; he had talent. A couple riders tried wearing catchers' masks to prevent facial injuries, but even that didn't work—Bo was just too ornery and dangerous to ride—so they retired him. Put him out to stud; he's a real happy camper now."

"I guess he was too smart for y'all," Justin states.

Sam laughs. "And his son Twister is mighty smart, too. That one kicks his heels higher than his head coming down from a jump and twists once or twice in the process. When a bull does that you know the rider is being jerked hard," then he adds quickly, "But your daddy will be okay; he's a great rider. You and your mom and dad going out tonight?"

"*Yep*," Justin grins. He loves evenings on the rodeo circuit. After dinner he and his parents go out for some boot scoot'n at a local country bar with a name like "The Watering Hole" or "The Feedlot" and no rules that ban kids if they came in with their parents.

The men wear cowboy boots made of lizard skin, ostrich, or python, and tight jeans and silk shirts and cowboy hats. The women wear cavalry jackets and suede shirts and pants or skirts trimmed in bone or beads.

Justin stays off the dance floor. There's too much happening out there. "It's easy, son," Bobby told him. "Half of the inside dance floor is for line dancing and free-style; the other half for swing dances. The outside lane, which circles the whole floor, is for the progressive dancers. They dance fast and serious. Stay out of their way or get trampled."

There's always a country-western band and a lot of stomping to the music—the Texas two-step, the Cotton-Eyed Joe and other line dances that make the floor vibrate as people dance in unison. And there's drinking and laughing and thick, cigarette smoke hanging in the air. Justin loves to inhale the smoky air. It gives him a little buzz.

"You better get back, your dad's up next," Sam smiles and gives him change for the ten dollars. Justin slips it into his pocket and starts back to the bleachers.

The voice on the loud speaker announces "Bobby Buller riding Twister!" The crowd cheers, and then gasps, and someone screams. Justin runs to the heavy, steel-pole fence at the sidelines. His daddy's thrown, but his hand is caught in the braided rope twisted around it. He struggles to free himself as the bull drags him around the arena.

The plate of ribs slip from Justin's hand and drop into the dirt. *No, no, nooo.* His daddy's arm is bent at an odd angle. Dorky Dinky Do runs in circles around Twister, and frantically waves a red flag and honks a horn, trying to distract the bull from his deadly assault. Twister swings his massive head around and knocks Dorky sprawling into the sawdust. Three men with long cattle prods move in on the animal to stun it and drive it back into the chute.

Justin slides between the fence poles and runs toward his daddy; did you lose your focus because I whined about being allowed to ride Mighty Bucky? If I hadn't whined, would you be okay?

37

Someone yells, "Get that damn kid out of here!" Justin dodges the hands that grab at him and runs out of their reach to watch from a distance as his daddy is loaded into an ambulance. The ground begins to shake like an earthquake; Justin turns to see Twister, who's broken free, thunder toward him.

Justin stands there paralyzed—terrified and helpless—and wets himself.

Suddenly the clown lounge rolls between the bull and Justin and a flash of red and purple streaks past him; Dorky! The bull slams into the barrel and then into Dorky, sending him flying, and behind the bull come half a dozen men on horseback who rope the bull so many times he can barely move any more.

Justin walks toward Dorky—slumped in the sawdust—and can't find the words to express his gratitude and love for Dorky. "Hey, lil' cowboy, I'm okay." He lays a shaky hand on Justin's arm, looks up into his eyes, and says evenly, "*Always* protect the people you love."

A guy with a towel runs up to Dorky and exclaims, "You're hurt bad, damn!"

Dorky tries to wave him away.

"No, man, here's your ear!" He unfolds the towel and shows Dorky his severed ear. Dorky turns his head and Justin gasps at a thick smear of blood that runs down the side of Dorky's head and onto his shirt.

Justin wretches, his legs collapse, he slumps to the ground and passes out.

7. "Now hear us"

"I'm going to play what each of us said, and then immediately after, play it in reverse," Luke told the group. "When it's in reverse, you'll hear gibberish and sounds at the ends of sentences like people sucking in their breath real fast. And every few seconds you'll hear speech reversals, words like forward speech, only faster with different accents on the syllables, so listen carefully. And, sometimes, there might not be any reversals."

"I'll write down any that we hear," Todd offered. Luke started the recording and there, in the thicket of the backward gibberish, small voices, *their* voices, called to whoever could hear them and understand.

> Luke: "What religions do we have here? I'm Methodist." **Play in the surf.**
>
> Nika: "Southern Baptist. Conservative."
>
> Todd: "Me, too—Southern Baptist—but a Moderate."
>
> Jon: "Jewish."
>
> Kim: "Buddhist."
>
> Ari: "Bahá'í. One of the world's fastest growing religions." **Whirl with it.**
>
> Jessica: "I don't have a name for my faith. Just a walk in the woods can be a spiritual experience." **He is my force, my oxygen.** "I guess you could say I believe in the God of nature."

Ari's astonishment shaded into alarm, then curiosity, and back to astonishment. And through it all she felt compelled to keep listening to that part of herself that had previously lived unheard in the remote regions of her mind. She shivered, Elaina crossed herself, and Nika whispered, "Even though I walk through the valley of the shadow of death Thou art with me."

Jon: "The Jews are still waiting for the Messiah."

Nika: "Jesus was the Messiah!" **I'm the angered wolf!** "The Bible says he was." **He was**.

Jon: "We think he was a great teacher, but not the Messiah." **Hear the lesson.** "Besides, the Bible isn't my holy book."

Todd: "Baptists are waiting for His second coming." **I love the Garden**.

Jon: "What do Bahá'ís believe?" **What? Tell**.

Ari: "We believe there's one spokesperson every 1,000 years or more to deliver God's message. The spokespeople so far have been Zoroaster, Buddha, Krishna, Moses, Jesus, Mohammed, and most recently Bahá'u'lláh, a Persian messenger of God in the 1800s." **God of Eden. I love Him**.

Nika: "So many? I think there was just one." **One**.

Todd: "So how do we know what's true?" **Scared of it**.

Ari: "Maybe when we play this recording backwards we'll find out." **Listen. Now hear us. Give us truth**.

"Well, there's matter and anti-matter, maybe there's a forward universe and a backward universe," Jon ventured, adjusting his glasses. "This is fascinating."

"I defend Jesus forwards *and* backwards," Nika grinned.

"It's poetry," Jessica said.

Todd smiled. "That's neat. In reverse I said **I love the Garden**, and Ari says the **God of Eden**. Do you suppose that means the Garden of Eden? And these speech reversals on Jessica, **He is my force, my oxygen** are like she's talking about God being her sustenance. We can't live without oxygen."

40

Ari was delighted at the wonder of it all. Maybe what was climbing "up and out" of their minds was coming from a greater Mind that they all shared in common regardless of race, religion, sex, or nationality. "Maybe we're moving closer to God," she said in awe. "Or God's moving closer to us."

"Or we're moving closer to the devil," Nika stated bluntly.

"*Ow ow*," Elaina exclaimed, "I have a cramp in my toe."

"That's because you've been twisting it," Todd said and playfully slapped her hand away from her sandals. "You've been twisting your toe ever since you sat down."

"You're going to give yourself arthritis when you get older," Nika said.

"Actually that's a myth," Kim corrected. "You can't get arthritis from cracking your knuckles and I assume you can't get it from twisting your toes, either."

"I'm sorry, I'm just nervous," Elaina apologized, sitting on her hands, and then urged, "Please keep going, let's hear some more."

Todd: "I don't want my speech reversals analyzed."
Homosexual.

The color drained from his face and Ari realized that it must be true, the rumor about him that was going around school. There was only one openly gay guy at school who was bullied mercilessly until he tried to kill himself and his parents took him out of school. No wonder Todd was still in the closet.

Todd braced for ridicule and avoided people's eyes.

"It's okay," Luke told him gently.

Jessica stated, "I'm a straight ally. I march in the Pride Parade in Dallas every year."

Ari sympathized with Todd. She thought, sometime I'll tell him how the kids at my school in Iran bullied me because my religion was different from the religion the government ordered us to believe; as if I could change what I know in my heart to be true.

"Can we not talk about this?" Todd asked, irritated.

"We won't tell anyone," Luke said, and then looked to the group for confirmation.

Jon, "Of course not."

Kim, "I won't tell."

Elaina, "No one will ever hear it from me."

Jessica, "I won't say anything. It's Todd's personal business."

Ari, "Mum's the word."

Silence.

"Nika?" Luke asked.

"What?"

"We're going to keep Todd's secret, right?"

"I guess so," she said and shrugged.

"I didn't expect this mind-reading machine to reveal *our* secrets," Luke said. "It makes sense, though. I guess it isn't choosey. It tells on everyone."

They all looked uncomfortable. At first Ari figured it was because they were embarrassed for Todd, but maybe they were all afraid that they'd tell on themselves as easily as Todd told on himself. Were they mentally sifting through their guilt looking for that one situation they most wanted to hide? She rubbed her throat. The only thing she wanted to hide, besides an understandable attraction to Luke, was an almost constant feeling of being vulnerable to the unexpected; well, there was that and the incident, the tragedy years ago—she shook her head to refuse the memory.

"I shoplifted a lipstick," Elaina blurted out, about to cry, "but I felt really bad about it and took it back the next day. Transylvania Red; that's what it was called."

"Transylvania Red would look real good on you, girl," Nika stated.

"Don't encourage her," Ari said, realizing how Elaina looked up to Nika.

"Who's encouraging her? All I said was that the color would look good on her—you know, with her dark skin—I'm not advocating a life of shoplifting," Nika said defensively.

The group fell silent, waiting for the next confession.

"Listen, if you think I'm going to admit to anything, you're wrong," Nika said. "I haven't done anything, ever, to be ashamed of."

"I smoked grass once," Kim said cautiously, "but it made my head feel blurry and muddled, and I want to stay sharp for Karate."

"I thought you were supposed to get all giddy and hungry on pot," Elaina said.

"I wouldn't know," Nika stated bluntly and Luke, Todd, Ari, and Jon followed with their own declarations of innocence, "Me neither," "I wouldn't know either," "Me neither," "I've just heard rumors."

"Well don't look at me," Jessica said, "I'm naturally spacey, or so I've been told."

"I wonder if they'll start doing speech reversal analysis on athletes as well as drug testing," Kim mused. His voice deepened to mimic a sports official, "Are you doing drugs? Please speak clearly into the recorder."

"I have a secret addiction," Jessica said. "I might as well tell you because it'll probably come out in my speech reversals." The kids leaned closer. She whispered, "I'm pretty health conscious, but I love that candy corn that people hand out at Halloween."

"Oh yeah," Elaina cried gleefully, "and those little marshmallow chicks at Easter, Little Peeps."

"I used to like those, too," Jessica said, "but marshmallow has gelatin in it, which comes from the skin, hooves, and bones of cows and pigs."

Elaina's eyes grew huge and teary so Nika quickly interjected, "I'd kill for chocolate."

Jon busied himself cleaning his glasses with the edge of his shirt.

"Hiding anything, Jon?" Luke joked.

Jon shook his head, nope.

Luke glanced at Todd, and then away. "Okay," he said, his deliberate tone barely masking his embarrassment for Todd. "Speech reversals can reveal people's secrets and seem to relate in some way to what's being said in a speaker's forward speech. This is a good example. Todd didn't want his speech reversals analyzed because, well, you know."

Todd sat silently, his jaw clenched.

"So if any of you, say, robbed a bank, just don't talk about crime in general," Luke advised, "talk about the weather, or something else, and you'll probably be okay."

"Sure is hot out today," Jon quipped and put his glasses back on.

"I hear it's going to be in the 90s," Ari added.

"I guess if we're going to do this work, we have to be willing to have our secrets exposed," Luke said, "and trust each other not to tell anyone. Can we do that?"

To Todd's relief, the group agreed quickly to strict confidentiality.

Ari thought that maybe it wouldn't be so bad to have Luke know what she was thinking. Imagine knowing someone that intimately. But she'd die of embarrassment if he knew that she was attracted to him; what would it be like if he kissed her? No! That was strictly forbidden in her culture between two people who weren't engaged or married. The mind-reading machine could prove to be very problematic. Well, she'd just have to distract herself and think about something other than kissing.

She never let anyone get close to her, anyway, under any circumstance. He looked up at her. She wondered if this mind-reading stuff was making them more sensitive to each other, possibly more intuitive.

They exchanged smiles. It comforted her to have someone share her new-found understanding that life was more complicated than they ever expected it would be, and more amazing than they previously imagined.

8. The Texas Tumbleweed

Sarah pulls into the parking lot of the Tumbleweed and parks. "Here's your new ID card," she says and passes it to Karen.

"You mean fake ID."

"*Shhh*, it's *new*, not 'fake.'"

"I never needed ID before," Karen says.

"They got a new bouncer. You never know. Some follow the rules, some don't. After a while, though, most of them relax a bit."

Karen studies the ID card, which says she's 21, but she looks young and clueless in the photo. She tells Sarah, "Flirt with the bouncer a little and maybe he'll let us in. You flirt better than anyone I know."

Sarah grins. "Sure, I'll flirt with him—that's a given—but just to increase our chances of getting by him, let's practice; show me your ID, casually, don't make a big deal about it. If you look self-conscious, that'll make him suspicious."

Karen shows her the card.

"No, no, you looked away. Okay, I'm the bouncer, look at me, smile pleasantly, casually, then look a little bored, and I'll say something to you and you look at me; that'll divert your attention from the bouncer to me. And don't clear your throat; it makes you look nervous."

Karen sighs heavily.

Sarah laughs. "You'll be fine."

Karen is an apt pupil, but still afraid to get caught trying to sneak into places.

"It's better to beg forgiveness than ask permission," Sarah states. "Okay, let's see your ID again."

They practice a couple more times and then Sarah gives the bouncer a big, sexy smile; he responds with an approving smile and looks her up and down. They flash their fake IDs at him, and while he's still under the influence of Sarah's smile, her short skirt, and her new Chocolate Lizard boots—he doesn't give Karen a second look—they stride past him into the bar. Sarah glances back at him over her shoulder and winks.

The man behind the bar calls to them, "Hey," pleased to see them.

"Hey, yourself, Andy," Sarah says and slides onto a barstool. "I'll have a frozen Margarita and make it a double with salt."

"Nice try, Sarah. No tequila for you. If I served that to you I'd be the one getting bounced—right out of my liquor license. You're underage and shouldn't even be in here."

"But you like us, we liven up the place. Now come on, Andy, please, a Margarita. Non-alcoholic drinks are so boring," she moans theatrically and drapes herself over the counter top.

"Yeah, boring," Karen echoes and slumps awkwardly across the counter top; it doesn't look as cool as when Sarah does it.

Sarah implores, "Just shake the bottle at the glass; maybe a *drop* of tequila will fall in."

"Nope, it's virgin drinks for you girls."

"Even if we're not?" Sarah says slyly and Karen blushes.

"Speak for yourself," Karen whispers. "I'm saving it 'till I get married."

"Oh, look, we've got company," Andy says as he hands them their non-alcoholic drinks.

Two middle-aged men stand in the doorway looking ill at ease. One wears a Hawaiian shirt, the other a shirt with a picture of a sailboat and the word "Skipper" written across it.

"I bet their boots are plastic," Karen says, proud of her new Slouch boots.

"Why don't you girls make Mauna Loa and Skipper feel welcome," Andy suggests. "I doubt anyone else is going to dance with them."

~~~

"*Ooops*," Mauna Loa says when he spills some of his drink on

46

the floor. Sarah, dancing next to him cringes and hands him a napkin, "You can clean it up with this. If you leave it, it'll make the floor slippery and then tacky when it dries; people won't be able to slide over it easily."

He does as he's told and then announces to all within ear shot, "Shouldn't you end the 'Electric Slide' with a brush kick instead of a hand clap? I saw it on You Tube and they were pretty specific."

"Who are you?" Sarah asks, marveling at how out of place he is.

"Me and my friend are in town on business, pretty lady," he answers and tips an imaginary cowboy hat.

A commotion prevents her from answering. Skipper, dancing with Karen, wander into the outer lane, where the fastest and best dancers are trying out their newest moves, and gets shoved out of the way.

"I need another drink," Mauna Loa says, "What are you ladies having?"

"Frozen Margaritas with salt, and make 'em doubles, thank yew," Sarah drawls and Karen turns away to hide a guilty smile. They were going to get their drinks after all—double strong.

It didn't take long for the girls to get a buzz on.

"I'm feeling really good," Sarah laughed, "Yee haw!" and Karen giggled.

Mauna Loa hands each of them another drink.

"Thank you, Mr. Mauna Loa," Sarah grins.

"Why'd you call me that?" he slurs.

"Mauna Loa is a Hawaiian volcano," Sarah says, sipping the drink, "and you look very tropical tonight."

"*Yeh*, and about to erupt, little lady," he drawls, pressing against her.

She winces, backs away, "Look, me and my friend want to dance with some of the other cowboys, too. We don't want to deprive anyone of our exquisite company."

The man's face darkens.

"I bet there are other ladies who'd love to dance with you,"

Sarah says, pointing him toward several women standing together at the bar. "Just remember, the dancers move counterclockwise, not clockwise, like you were trying to do earlier. And when a dance is over, don't stand there socializing. Get off the dance floor." She nudges him toward the women.

Sarah's assertiveness inspires Karen to disentangle herself from Skipper who's draped around her. "I'm going to go powder my nose."

But instead of asking someone else to dance, Mauna Loa and Skipper watch Karen and Sarah head toward the ladies' room.

"I don't know about you," Mauna Loa says, "but I think we've been given the brush off, and that isn't polite."

"I know what you mean," Skipper agrees. "I don't like it either."

They stand there, drinks in hand, and mull over what to do.

"I think they need to be taught some manners," Mauna Loa says.

9. Kenny/Joe

Moonlight seeps through the thin, tattered curtains of the trailer, spreads softly across the empty beer cans scattered across the floor, and dimly lights Kenny's flushed face. Rusty snores loudly in a chair. He jerks awake, momentarily confused as to where he is, then remembers, smacks his lips. The clock says 1:45 a.m.

Kenny opens an eye, scratches his belly, sniffs, "*Phew*, something stinks."

"I hate to tell you this, my friend, but that'd be you," Rusty points out.

Kenny stretches and searches through a pile of rubbish on the coffee table. When he finds his half-eaten burger, he chomps into it.

"Hey, you going to church this morning," Rusty jokes, "to atone for your sins?"

Kenny speaks through a mouthful of burger, "I am at church. I'm worshipping at the shrine of the holy cow." He laughs and spatters bits of lettuce onto his stomach. He wipes his mouth with his forearm, "Karen, get out here and make me some coffee."

"She's not your servant."

"She owes me," Kenny growls. "I feed her sorry butt and keep a roof over her head."

"It's way too early for coffee. Go back to sleep. You need your beauty rest."

"My head's spinning, I'm dry as a desert, and I don't give a dang what time it is, I want Karen to get me some coffee!"

"Her bedroom door's open. I don't think she's here."

"KAREN!" Kenny bellows, and then, "I've got a freakin' hangover and you refuse to make me coffee." He picks at the corner of his nose and pouts, his voice softer now, "Karen, get me some coffee," but he knows he's talking to himself. She isn't there to obey.

His jaw tightens. Where is that ungrateful girl? He saw things in Iraq no one should ever have to see and all Karen did was have fun while he paid the bills for her. She has no idea the things that go on in the world. Anger squeezes him from the inside like a convulsion; he begins to pant as though he's been running a long way, like he's possessed and wants to wring someone's neck. His anger resembles what a shrink on a TV talk show had called a "rage disorder." He writes down new words when he hears them on TV so he can enlarge his vocabulary and better himself. Karen wasn't going to be the only one in the family with an education, so he wrote down "rage disorder" when he heard it on TV. *Yep*, that's me, all right—unpredictable and explosive—and I'm damn proud of it.

"No wonder I'm upset, Rusty. Life's treating me stinkin' rotten, and instead of being helpful, that *la-di-dah* Karen disapproves of me. She's always saying snotty things like, 'You shouldn't shoot squirrels and possums just for sport,' and I tell her, 'Well, why not? They take up too much room in the forest.'" He chuckles. "And when she gripes about me littering I tell her, 'I'm creating jobs for people. Road crews get hired to pick up the stuff, but then she says in that *la-di-dah* voice of hers, 'Then why don't you take a grammar course and give a teacher a job?'"

"Having a good time making yourself miserable, my friend?" Rusty asks.

"That Karen is so *la-di-dah*, putting me down, thinking she's so educated. She's just a junior in high school. Just 'cause I didn't finish school don't mean I'm not smart. I have street smarts, and other smarts, too. Psychic smarts. Sometimes I see lights in my head while I'm bass fishing and I know what's going to happen later that day like my boss is going to do something stupid or the store will be out of cigarettes. I told Karen that I saw psychic lights flashing in my head, and you know what she said, she said, 'What you're having is a stroke from eating too many burgers.' She's so disrespectful. She needs to learn some respect."

"Listen, we can go out for breakfast at the Get 'n' Go when it opens. You need something more than a stale burger and a quart of tequila in your stomach."

"What I need is Karen to get home and make me some coffee."

"You're always griping about her."

"Sibling rivalry." "Sibling" was another word he learned from TV.

"Naw, it's more than that."

"She's stupid and I hate stupid people," Kenny sputters, "She's a bitter disappointment."

"I think she has a good head on her shoulders."

"You like her, don't ya? You've got the hots for my sister!"

"We've gone out a couple times. That's more proof she's smart, going out with me, and she's going to graduate from high school in a couple years."

"An education isn't everything," Kenny fumes.

"You jealous of her because she's happy and you're not?"

Kenny scowls while Rusty looks for a clean cup in the kitchen and settles for a used one with a lipstick print on the rim. He runs tap water into it, tops it off with a teaspoon of instant coffee, and sets it in the microwave to heat. "Karen will graduate, get a boyfriend, me or someone else, and move out of this crummy place and leave you."

That was the wrong thing to say. Kenny sees terrible pictures of himself in his mind: passed out on the smelly couch with no one ever getting him coffee and Karen out somewhere having a good time, a *la-di-dah* good time, laughing at him. Her laughter echoes in his head.

"Stop ragging on her and have some coffee," Rusty says and holds out the cup to him. He sees the lipstick print on the rim leering at him and knocks it out of Rusty's hand.

"Hey!" Rusty shouts, "I'm outta here, man. Call me if you get out of this stinking mood." He slams the door behind him.

Kenny starts to shake. He begins to count: one, my ma left me when she died; two, my dad left me; three, Karen left me; four, Rusty left me. Four people. Now I'm alone. I'm too good a guy for everyone to treat me so rotten. People are *ALWAYS* pushing my buttons. I'd be happy if they wouldn't push my buttons. They're going to make me do something I don't want to do—they'll bring it on themselves.

Pain jabs him in the head and a feeling creeps through him like slow, hot lava. He goes rigid with rage from head to toe, stumbles into the kitchen and kicks the cupboard door under the sink so hard it springs open, daring him to kick it again, so he does. Things—like the door—*always* defy him when he's in one of his moods. He kicks the cupboard door again and hurts his foot. The pain enrages him. Karen made me hurt my frickin' foot! Karen used to care about me, or *pretend* to care because I pay the bills. She tried to talk me out of my moods and wondered why I hated her so much, and she'd say I had "stinkin' thinking" and needed a "check up from the neck up." But now she's lost interest in me. Well, I won't be ignored.

He storms into the back bedroom, retrieves his Glock from the nightstand. He places a tender kiss on the barrel; his only friend. His breathing is shallow, cheeks numb, nostrils flare and the whites of his eyes are bright half moons under each pupil. The gun feels good in his hand. The gun can speak for him. His bad mood is so strong it has a life of its own. "Joe." The dark mood seems to be a "Joe." Joe is upon him now something fierce. Adrenaline pumps in his veins, his blood pressure rises and inflames his cheeks, bile leaks into his stomach—he burps. He needs relief. Just before his vision goes gray, he growls, "Let's go find those girls."

10. "Hear me, man, don't hear Satan"

"This place is great," Jon exclaimed as Luke opened the door to his family's lake house and invited him, Nika, Kim, and Ari in.

The house had high, beamed ceilings, a large living room with a polished, wooden floor and a three-sided fireplace. They walked out onto a wooden deck that ran the entire length of the house, which faced a green meadow that sloped gently to the water's edge. The water was quiet, silky, and darker where the lake was the deepest. Ari inhaled the fragrance of early wildflowers: bluebonnets. "It's so peaceful," she said, "we should meet here all the time."

"Nope," Luke said, "my parents are in and out too much. We couldn't count on having the place to ourselves. They're gone today. I promised I wouldn't have a wild party."

Ari gave a little laugh. The group was here for something about as far from a party as you could get. They were here on serious business: to read minds.

They dressed casually—shorts and jeans and t-shirts—but Ari took a little extra care to look especially nice for Luke. She was wearing a sleeveless, racerback tank top tucked into low-waist dark brown shorts. The lemon color of the tank top set off her olive skin nicely. She tossed her hair casually back off her shoulders. Luke was wearing jeans and a work shirt. Boys had it so easy. Just throw anything on and they were good to go.

"I bet you see a lot of stars out here at night," Jon said, "great for astrophotography. On a dark night you can see the Andromeda Galaxy with the naked eye. The light we see left that galaxy more than two million years ago; it might not even be there any more."

"You're photographing the distant past," Jessica marveled.

"You can come out here some night and set up your camera equipment," Luke invited and Jon eagerly accepted.

Ari studied Jon's high forehead and wondered if it were true what she'd heard that high foreheads indicated superior intelligence.

"*Ewww*, what's that?" Luke asked as he peered into a carton of something Jessica brought with her for lunch.

"Hamburger Helper made with tofu instead of meat," she answered. She stuck a plastic fork in and pulled out a white chunk of something smeared with yellow goo. "Want some?"

Luke shuddered, "I'll pass. I prefer rib-eye steaks."

"I want tofu," Kim said optimistically. He took the tofu off the end of her fork with his fingers and ate it. "Hey, that's good."

When Luke and Ari burst out laughing Kim insisted, "No, it really is. I'm always looking for new ways to fix tofu."

"Yeah, me, too," Ari said with friendly sarcasm.

"Oh, you unfortunate souls who eat meat," Jessica lamented, "We'll see what sad shape your arteries are in 10 years from now, not to mention your conscience, eating living creatures."

"Actually, they're dead when I eat them," Luke said.

"Not funny," Jessica said sternly, "You know what I mean."

"My arteries will be squeaky clean," Kim declared, "as will my conscience."

Ari studied Jessica with her creamy, flawless complexion, gorgeous cascading strawberry-blonde hair, and slender figure. Then she looked at Kim, cheerful, confident, and physically fit. If these were what vegetarians looked like, "I'll try a bite," she said and Jessica happily handed her a piece.

"Not bad," Ari commented, "and not particularly good, either."

The doorbell rang and Luke let Todd and Elaina in. When they sat down he handed Elaina a Tablet. "You can keep it. You're the only one in the group who didn't have a tablet, iPad, or iPhone and we need them for our work. I loaded the latest assignment."

Elaina looked incredulous as she hesitantly accepted the slim tablet. She whispered, "These cost a lot of money."

"It wasn't that expensive," Luke said.

"In whose world?" Elaina wondered. "But okay, if you say so. Thank you."

Luke asked, "Okay, did everyone get the sound files on people in the news a while back that I emailed you? While you're pulling those up, would you help me get the drinks, Ari?" They filled the orders—sparkling mineral water for Jessica and Kim, lemonade for Nika, Todd, Jon, Luke, and Elaina, and iced herbal tea with lemon for Ari. Then they all settled comfortably into the living room, spread out their notes, and kicked off shoes and sandals.

"Okay, practice assignments. Who wants to start?" Luke asked.

"We will," Jessica volunteered. "Jon, Elaina, and I studied a couple televangelists who were involved in scandals a few years back. We found this on one of them who preached high moral standards, but then got caught keeping company with 'ladies of the night,' to put it politely. Here's his speech reversal as he sobbed his confession to the media, **I have sinned, I must admit in my mind**."

Elaina added, "The second guy was accused of throwing prayer requests into a dumpster after taking the checks out of the envelopes. When he was confronted about it, he insisted that he prayed over the requests before he threw them away, but his reversal contradicted him: **Forgive me**."

"So the televangelists are guilty, I guess," Todd said, "or at least ethically challenged."

"It looks that way," Luke said, "but you'd probably need more proof than just their reversals. I doubt that it'd be acceptable evidence in court."

"I wonder what reversals we'd find on televangelists who preach so adamantly against gays," Todd said under his breath and more to himself than to the others. They all looked at him. He added, "Some of those guys were caught *not* practicing what they preach."

Jessica agreed, "Reversal analysis could certainly expose people's hypocrisy. It might be fun to hear what they're really thinking."

"And it shows when they believe what they're saying," Luke said. "Here's a speech reversal on a gospel singer, **hear me, man, don't hear Satan**."

Kathleen L. Hawkins

"Here are some I found," Kim said. "They're on a cult leader in Waco, Texas, who was holed up with his followers in a compound that federal agents eventually stormed. The guy said, **don't want to kill. I am nervous. I feel afraid**. He was ready to die for his faith, though, given no other alternatives, **let me warn you. Arm the people**. He also said in reverse, **Jesus wants a harem**, a particularly interesting reversal because the guy was reported to think that he was the second coming of Jesus Christ and had the right to be involved intimately with a number of young women in the group."

Nika shuddered.

"Nika, who'd you analyze?" Luke asked.

"No one; we shouldn't be doing this."

"I have someone," Ari stated eagerly, ignoring Nika's concerns, "and this is chilling. There was a football star accused of killing his wife and her friend, and later acquitted. In the beginning the judge asked the suspect if he understood that they extended the date to start jury selection. The reversal on the judge was **he killed them**."

Kim sucked in his breath. "So the judge thought he was guilty *before* the trial started. Judges are supposed to be impartial."

"Everyone has opinions," Todd stated. "Judges just have to keep theirs to themselves, and that used to be possible until speech reversal analysis."

Ari continued. "When the suspect told the judge that he understood what the judge said about a speedy trial, his speech reversal was, **I killed them**. Then the judge asked if that arrangement was agreeable, and the judge's reversal was, **He killed lady love**. Oh, and get this. After the suspect was acquitted he told an interviewer, 'The worse thing that you can ever have, is have your argument taped. I would say anyone that's out there that's married and in a relationship just turn a tape recorder on the next time you have an argument and play it back, you will not believe that was you. **I skinned them all**.'"

Jon, who was familiar with the case, stated "He didn't skin the victims, he cut their throats."

56

Nika interpreted the reversal for him. "The suspect was black; the word "skinned" is slang for conned."

Luke said enthusiastically, "See that validates my instinct to have a diverse make-up in our group. If Nika weren't one of us, we wouldn't have the benefit of her unique interpretation."

"So the suspect fooled them all," Jon said, "maybe referring to the jury or the TV audience."

"Maybe he got away with murder and his unconscious mind communicated that fact," Luke said.

The sound of the pulse in Ari's ears was like someone inside her knocking, wanting to get out. Confessions in reverse; this could change the way trials are run, change the whole court system. Detectives might have an easier job proving guilt or innocence and trials could be over faster. She wondered what lawyers were going to think of this.

Luke reminded them again, "Speech reversals *suggest* guilt or innocence. The reversals might not be totally conclusive. We have to learn a lot more about this phenomenon."

Ari considered the immensity of it—they heard the private thoughts of a murderer—and she felt totally incapable emotionally of dealing with death, either forward or in reverse. When she thought about it, really thought about it, murder was ghastly, revolting, and grisly. People are used to seeing sanitized versions of it on TV and in the movies. When people bleed in the movies, it's fake blood: corn syrup mixed with red dye and a little chocolate syrup. But they were listening to the real thing. **I killed them**. Adding to her dismay was her new-found knowledge of exactly how deep rage could go for some people, how deeply rooted it was in their psyches. "We're witnessing crime as no one else ever has before," she marveled, "from the insides of people's heads. I'm going to need therapy after hearing how low some people sink."

Luke nodded and held her gaze. They were intimately connected by this thing they were doing, this speech analysis. The space between them in the room seemed to collapse. She could feel him against her, the rough fabric of his work shirt, his muscles through the shirt, his breath on her cheek. She felt him holding her close, needing her. They were part of each other, inseparable. Were these thoughts his or hers? Were they all thinking with one mind? It was as if some little kid was slowly erasing the lines between stick figures in a drawing, and everything that separated them was falling away: race, color, creed, gender, sexual orientation.

Luke closed his eyes and Ari imagined that he did it to better visualize her without all the group distraction. Was he thinking about her? She often closed her eyes to shut out the world and bring him to mind. She'd see that generous smile of his that put people at ease and the way he leaned forward to claim someone's attention, or nodded while they were talking. He was comfortable with people. She loved that about him. But now, was he trying to hide his feelings for the work they were doing? Was he scared, maybe for the first time in his easy, sheltered life?

She felt woozy with what she was feeling about reading people's minds. Her head swam with the inner voices of televangelists, a misguided cult leader who thought he was the second coming of Jesus Christ, and a suspected murderer—and the sky darkened outside, lights winked on around the lake, and the song of a Whippoorwill was muted by the sound of her own thoughts, fears, and questions growing louder and louder in her ears, thundering.

11. Justin Buller

Police Chief Justin Buller sits at his desk, slurps coffee, and scowls at a manila folder. His secretary, Inez, sits across from him.

"Is that the missing persons report, the girls?" she asks.

"Yes. Gone three days, car abandoned out on Highway 733. We'll have to clear my schedule. What have we got this week?"

"On Tuesday, your talk at the high school about drug and alcohol abuse. Wednesday and Thursday interview people for the new detective position. Friday you're taping the YouTube video to show homeowners how to burglar proof their homes."

"Move everything back a week. Is the ghost car parked at the Get 'n' Go today?"

She nods yes.

Bull adds proudly, "The sight of that police cruiser slows down speeders. They don't know if there's anyone in it. We haven't issued any speeding tickets this year. And letting the officers drive the cruisers home keeps a high police profile in town."

"Spirit Mound is crime free compared to other towns. It's eerie."

"It *was* crime free until these girls went missing. Have Hank impound the abandoned car. I'm going to check the places they were last seen, interview people who talked to them, look at security videos." He was silent, deep in thought. "I have an uneasy feeling."

"Radio? Maybe some music will help you relax."

He nods, she turns on the radio, leaves the office.

A plaintive country-western singer cautions, "Mamas, don't let your babies grow up to be cowboys. Don't let 'em pick guitars and drive them old trucks. Make 'em be doctors and lawyers and such …" and transports him back to the hospital room that terrible day when he sat quietly in a metal chair in the corner while his daddy lay bandaged in bed.

Twister did it. The thing was, though, bulls were often mild-mannered before and after an event. They turned mean—or maybe frantic—when a strap was tightened around their flanks and they were prodded and antagonized into bucking. He'd sure object if someone did that to him, but what was it his daddy taught him to say? "The strap doesn't hurt the animal; it just gives him the incentive to buck hard and effectively."

In any case, Twister dragged Bobby as Dorky Dinky Do heroically tried to distract him and when Bobby finally pulled free of the rope and fell to the ground, the furious bull trampled him and dislocated one of his kneecaps.

When Bobby was taken to the emergency room and washed down, the doctors said that his skin looked like someone went after him with a saw-toothed blade. And the way he was coughing, wheezing, and gagging, he probably inhaled a bunch of sawdust in the arena as well.

Sally paced by the bed and told him, "They say you'll live, baby, but you'll be in pain. This wouldn't have happened, Bobby, if you stayed put like I wanted you to, but *nooo*, you had to run all over creation on the rodeo circuit and take us with you. You were never happy in any one place, were you?"

Justin jiggled his feet in his pointy-toed cowboy boots and worried silently. Daddy, you needed to focus on riding Twister, but I pestered you to let me ride Mighty Bucky at rodeo school. Did you lose your focus and get hurt because of me?

Sally grew impatient. "Bobby, I've tried to be supportive, but I've had it. I can't believe you'd want to continue on the circuit. You probably can't ride any more. All you'll be good for is mucking out stalls or serving up barbecue at a food booth like Sam. Is that the life you want?"

Bobby wheezed an incomprehensible reply from under the bandages.

"Does that mean 'yes'?" she asked. "Are you going to keep on with the rodeo?"

Bobby sighed, coughed, whispered, "I love it, baby."

"Justin's going to need a stable life now that school's starting in a couple weeks." She sank into a chair beside Bobby, rested her forehead on his arm. "Honey, I want to stay with you, but Justin has to start first grade. We're going to go live with Mom in Spirit Mound. I'll get a job, Mom will look after him while I work, and you can join us when you feel better. Please say you'll join us when you can."

Silence.

"I guess that says it all." She stood up, went to the door, turned back slowly, and sighed, "Okay then, Justin, say good-bye to your father."

He stood up, tucked in his shirt, approached Bobby, and said gently. "G'bye, daddy."

~~~

His dad never joined them in Spirit Mound and when the postcards stopped coming Sally wouldn't find out why. "It'd hurt too much," she told Justin. "I'd rather think that your daddy recovered enough to ride again and is off somewhere living his dream."

When Justin told his father, "G'bye, daddy," that night in the hospital he didn't know how painful grief could be or how long forever was.

~~~

Spirit Mound, a small country town in North Central Texas— named after a sacred Native American gathering site during the early pioneer days—bordered Spirit Lake. When Justin and his mom pulled into Spirit Mound—towing their belongings in a U-Haul—the first thing they saw was a huge flock of geese flying across the face of the sun. They must have been resting on the lake before they continued their migration. The sight of the flock flying as though they shared one mind, inspired by a single thought, took Justin's breath away. He watched them fly gracefully in formation, compelled by a mysterious, inner drive. It was then he knew that Spirit Mound was enchanted. His daddy was taken from him and in his place, this bewitched, wonderful town. It should have been called Magic Mound.

~~~

"Bull" was Justin's nickname at the police academy. He grew into a tall, heavy-set man—without being fat—and a bull ruined his daddy's rodeo career, so the name fit.

After he graduated from the academy he returned to Spirit Mound and claimed it as his own by first taking a job as a beat cop, and then working his way up through the ranks to police chief. His daddy's drifter lifestyle left a bad impression on him. It crippled the cowboy, ended his marriage, and stole a father from his son. Bull was determined to live life differently, to stay in one place and protect the town and never let it down. He took Dorky's advice seriously, "*Always* protect the people you love." So Bull focused on the safety of Spirit Mound and its citizens, and that focus never wavered. There'd be no crime in Spirit Mound. He wouldn't allow it. Zero tolerance.

He was into crime prevention big time. He spoke at schools against drug and alcohol abuse, told homeowners how to burglar proof their homes, and parked an empty police cruiser at different locations each day to deter crime and discourage speeders. His deputy, Hank Cooper, followed him to the selected spot for the day; Bull parked the car and rode back with Hank. He tied a coyote tail to the antenna of his own cruiser so people would know it was his and be especially careful.

He did his job so well that there was practically nothing for law enforcement to do in Spirit Mound. Occasionally a high school kid drank too much, a serious situation, granted, but infrequent. Spirit Mound was crime free, until two girls went missing.

This case was going to test him. It might be as simple as two kids having spent the weekend away from home and they'd turn up, defiant, and ready to face their parents and the consequences, but somehow he didn't think he was that lucky.

He opens his desk drawer and takes out an old, grainy postcard of a clown snagged through the belt loop on the horn of a bull and lifted off the ground. The clown dangles in the air and looks like he's trying to swim away from the bull. It reminds Justin of Dorky who used to say, "It's not *whether* you're gonna get hurt, but when and how bad." Dorky's ear was reattached, but never looked quite right after that; it looked like a dried apricot.

Bull picks up a second postcard, his favorite: a huge bull tossed a rider over its horns and the cowboy was headed straight for the ground, his arms outstretched to break his fall, but through the magic of photography, he never hit the ground. He remained forever suspended in time in mid-air.

I imagine this is you, Daddy, never hitting the ground, forever safe. You didn't come back to us after you got hurt at the rodeo, but maybe you recovered enough to ride again and you're off somewhere living your dream. I loved you, the way you talked to me like you respected me—not in that sing-song voice a lot of grownups use on babies—and when Mom slept in we'd go to Chubby's Café for biscuits and gravy, bacon and eggs, just you and me.

He sighs fondly. Rodeos were thrilling in those days, the bulls dangerous, the ribs fragrant and tasty, the bands lively and loud, and little boys could go into crowded, smoke-filled bars with their parents and watch country-western dancing. But then his daddy was trampled at the rodeo and everything changed.

He puts the postcards back in the desk drawer next to his gleaming 45-calibre pistol and, next to that, a bag of chocolates with creamy centers. He eats a handful.

12. "I feel nasty weather"

The clean cut, college-age server surveyed the group of kids seated in his section for dinner at the Pizza Palace. They were wearing a variety of styles and colors: bold African prints, soft plaids, denim, western wear, and a Karate outfit with a black belt. Being near Dallas, Spirit Mound had a lot of diversity, but it was unusual to see a group of such racially mixed kids hang out together.

He took their orders then asked, "You guys with the Foreign Language Club?"

Kim laughed, "Yeah, we study a foreign language," but having been sworn to secrecy about The Insiders, he didn't specify that they studied the language of the unconscious mind. The server looked puzzled and left.

"Our next assignment, should you choose to accept," Luke said and slid a poster across the table with photos of the missing girls: Karen and Sarah. Under the photos were the words: Last seen at The Texas Tumbleweed Bar. Reward: $10,000 for information leading to an arrest. Call (817) 555-1213.

"Wow, we could make money analyzing speech reversals?" Todd exclaimed. "Ten thousand dollars."

"I'm in," Jessica said and the others nodded.

"I recorded a segment on the 5 o'clock news," Luke said, "and emailed each of you the sound file; here's the transcript." He handed everyone a sheet of paper. "It's a reporter questioning Andy Snyder, the owner of The Texas Tumbleweed, and then a comment by Police Chief Buller. The reversals are in bold print."

Andy: "Yeah, they were here most the evening." **Hot girls**.

Reporter: "What time did they leave?"

Andy: "About 2:10."

Reporter: "Doesn't the bar close at two?"

Andy: "Yeah, but I let 'em stay while I was cleaning up." **I want you, honey, Sarah**.

Reporter: "Was anyone with them while you were cleaning up?"

Andy: "Nope, just me and them." **I'm a sexy warrior**.

Reporter: "So they didn't leave with anyone?"

Andy: "Not that I know of. I went in the back for a few minutes and when I came back out they were gone." **They go**. "They spent some time dancing with a guy in a Hawaiian shirt and his friend, but the guys left when the bar closed."

Reporter: "Chief Buller, do you suspect foul play?" **Do you?**

Bull: "Sorry, I can't comment on that at this time." **I feel nasty weather**.

Reporter: "Here's what we saw when we studied the security video from the bar." **Saw it**.

Video: the bar is empty except for two girls who look around to make sure no one is looking, finish off a few drinks that people left on the counter, and then leave the bar together.

Andy: "I did not give them any booze!" **Not**. "Anyway, maybe Hawaiian guy and his friend were waiting for them in the parking lot."

Reporter to the audience: "The bar owner is referring to a customer who was wearing a Hawaiian shirt. If any of our viewers might know who 'Hawaiian guy' is, please call the Spirit Mound police station and ask for Chief Buller. And that's it for now. We'll update you as we learn more." **Later**.

"The bar owner thinks he's a real stud," Jessica said, "but I don't think he hurt anyone. He said **they go**, not 'we go,' which suggests that he didn't leave with the girls; the security video validates that. He's telling the truth."

Luke agreed. "It said later on the news that customers said the girls were tipsy so Chief Buller booked the bar owner for serving liquor to minors. He swears he didn't give them any, but it was illegal for the bar owner to let them in, in the first place. Now here's an interesting news segment with Kenny, the half brother of one of the girls."

Kenny (to the reporter): "Why'd you question the trailer park manager? That man has no idea what he's talking about. He hardly knew Karen. He hasn't owned the trailer park very long." **Shot 'em. Rocks weigh down the sack. Mask sis.** "Why would anyone want to harm my sister and her friend? There's no reason they'd want to do that. I was with my friend Joe that evening." **Joe serves this howl**.

"And here's a segment with Kenny's friend Rusty," Luke said.

Rusty: "Me and Karen dated some and I knew Sarah pretty good." **Their death is asleep. Ruin them.** "People are calling in with all these ideas about what might have happened to them, suggesting where they might be and that just irks me. They probably just ran off for a while." **He shot 'em. I'm a sender. Are dead. Suggestion, rough the scenery**.

"Kenny sounds guilty of *murder*," Todd exclaimed, "Rusty saw it and helped Kenny cover his tracks: **suggestion, rough the scenery**. Rusty is a **sender**, a messenger. His speech reversals are telling on Kenny, but maybe he doesn't want to tell the police because they might arrest him as an accomplice."

"The bar owner shouldn't be in jail," Elaina added. "Bull's wasting his time on the wrong guy; he should go after Kenny."

"'Bull'?" Luke asked.

"That's Chief Buller's nickname."

Luke nodded, "Okay, then, Bull it is. Now, moving on, **rocks weigh down sack.**"

"Kenny shot the girls," Kim speculated, "put them in sacks, and dumped them in a lake or river or a stock pond."

"Great, let's claim the reward," Elaina exclaimed. "Call Bull."

"Wait, not so fast," Luke said. "We want to be absolutely sure we get credit for solving the case. This recording has to lead to a conviction. I'm not sure that we have enough evidence, yet, and I don't know if a confession in reverse would be accepted in court."

"There's no precedent," Jon stated. "No one has ever entered speech reversals as evidence that I know of."

"How about calling Bull anonymously and telling him he's got the wrong man," Ari suggested, "and then call him again and tempt him with a little more information. Parcel it out so he has to depend on us. He'll be waiting for our calls."

"I like the way you think," Luke told her.

"My aunt Inez is Bull's secretary," Elaina said. "I have the number of the police station in case I need to call her at work." She showed Luke the number to call from his phone.

"Whoa, wait a minute" Jon said quickly, "Bull will see your caller ID."

"There's a pay phone in the hall by the restrooms," Jessica said. "Call him from there."

"What is this thing of which you speak, a 'pay phone'?" Elaina teased.

Jessica rolled her eyes and played along, "Oh, the younger generation. A pay phone, my young friend, is a phone for the public to use that takes coins."

"Okay, pay phone it is," Luke said and glanced around the restaurant to see if anyone was eavesdropping on them. It was still early and the only other customer was a woman arguing with a little boy who was demanding money to play video games in the back of the restaurant.

"So Bull can't trace the call from a pay phone?" Todd asked.

"I don't know, but keep it short just to be safe," Jessica said.

Luke dialed and asked for the police chief. "Hi Chief Buller, I'm with The Insiders investigative group."

Ari's eyebrows shot up, surprised and pleased. They had a name like a real company.

"We have information about the missing girls, Karen and Sarah," Luke continued. "We think Kenny killed them, his friend Rusty witnessed it, and the owner of the bar is innocent."

There was silence on the other end of the line, then Bull stated, "We considered Kenny a person of interest—he's known around town to have volatility issues—so we talked to him and let him go."

Jon drew his finger across his throat to signal Luke to cut the call short. He nodded and summarized, "Don't waste your time on the bar owner or looking for the guy in the Hawaiian shirt who was at the bar; question Kenny again. Talk soon." He ended the call and told the group, "Kenny told the reporter that he was with someone named Joe. And if Rusty was there, too, there might be three of them involved. I think we need more evidence."

"But look at everything we've learned," Ari said. "We know the suspect is probably innocent, who the murderer is and how he killed them, where he hid the bodies—in water—and who might have seen it or helped cover it up; all that from a few statements on the news."

"Think of the great information we could get if we had a recording of Bull questioning Kenny at length," Luke said.

"Bull records interviews with suspects," Elaina offered, "and my aunt transcribes them."

"Great," Luke exclaimed. "Can you get us a copy of the Kenny recording?"

"Oh no," Elaina protested. "My aunt wouldn't just give it to me, especially if I told her that we wanted to play it backwards to read a guy's mind. Do you know how crazy that sounds?"

"Then we can't go any farther with this case," Luke said.

"And the girls won't be avenged," Nika added, shaking her head sadly.

"They might convict the wrong man for the murders," Kim stated, "He could get the death penalty, which is popular here in Texas."

"And the bad guy will get away," Jessica said. "What if he's a serial killer? No one will be safe. And what if he branches out and starts to kill people in other towns?"

"And we can kiss the ten grand good-bye," Todd added, miffed.

"Okay, I'll try to get a copy of the interrogation," Elaina relented. "*Jeeze*, you make it sound like I'm going to save the world. Luke, will you order me a small pizza with pepperoni to go? I have an idea."

13. "Sin is shallow"

Ari leapt out of bed, excited about the day's possibilities: seeing Luke again, having lunch with new friends, exploring reversals, maybe solving a murder and collecting the reward. She laughed as she showered and wondered how many people had a to-do list like hers.

She dried off, ran her fingers through her dark hair to give it a tousled look, put on makeup, and slipped into a pair tight fitting jeans and a form-fitting black t-shirt with a V-neck. She finished off the look with her favorite necklace with the onyx heart and a touch of sandalwood perfume on each wrist. She turned in front of the mirror, imagined her through Luke's eyes, then grabbed her sandals and ran downstairs barefoot.

It was all her mother, Maryam, could do to get her to slow down long enough to eat breakfast. "Tell me about these new friends of yours," she quizzed as she set a bowl on the table in front of her. Ari peered into it and wrinkled her nose, "*Ewww*, oatmeal."

"Just eat it, it's good for you," Maryam scolded, "and tell me about your friends."

Ari tried not to fight her mother when she cross-examined her; it was her mom's worry talking, left over from living in Iran where people were snatched up and disappeared, where one was leery of strangers and suspicious of friends who could pump you subtly for information about your family's religious activities and report you if you didn't obey the law. After the incident in second grade when the teacher tricked Ari into admitting she was a Bahá'í and encouraged the other girls to torment her, Maryam and Ari stopped talking about their personal lives and guarded their thoughts carefully. Being cautious became a habit.

America had dangers of its own Ari discovered. There might be a murderer loose in Spirit Mound and only a matter of time before

The Insiders ran smack into him. He might be sitting at the next table in a restaurant or standing behind them at the cash register in a store, secure in the fact that he looked ordinary.

"They're just kids from school, Mom," then thinking to herself, we sit around and eavesdrop on a killer. It really scares me, listening to the thoughts of a killer.

"There's something you're not telling me," Maryam said. "You look worried, Arianna."

"I'm fine."

"My intuition says you're *not*."

Ari noticed how her mother's flowered spring dress accentuated her slim, petite figure. "You look nice today, Mom." It was a relief that neither of them had to wear the long, loose clothing that the government in Iran mandated that women wear.

Maryam's eyes narrowed "Don't change the subject," and she pulled up a chair to sit next to her daughter.

"*Uh oh*, I see this on cop shows," Ari complained. "All that's missing is a video camera and a glaring light bulb overhead."

"That's where I learn my interrogation techniques," Maryam said, "from cop shows on TV. I also know how to do brain surgery from watching doctor shows."

Ari laughed. "I'm lucky I don't need brain surgery." She looked directly at her mother to give the impression she wasn't hiding anything. Sitting this close, she noticed the frown lines between her mom's eyebrows; lines etched in Iran and deepened in America, and would probably never go away.

"I have to go to work," Maryam said, "and it'd help me to know that you aren't going to get into any trouble."

"Mom, I get good grades, I don't smoke or do drugs, and I come home at night when I'm told to. Now that I think about it, I sound pretty lame."

"There's no shame in being a good student, you should be very proud—I'm proud of you—but I'm still not convinced that everything is okay."

"Believe it, everything's fine. We're just working on a project."

"A science project, an experiment?"

"Sort of."

"Tell me about it."

"You're going to be late for work."

Maryam glanced at her watch and sighed, "Okay, but I want to hear about it when I get home tonight. And I want to meet your friends. I'm going to be all over you like ducks on a June bug."

Ari smiled. Her mother tried to incorporate Texas sayings and idioms whenever possible, but they seemed out of place when a Persian woman said them.

Ari rinsed her dish and put it in the dishwasher. She was eager to listen again to the sound file that Luke made of the TV interview—to see if she could ferret out any reversals the other kids missed before she met them for lunch.

~~~

"You're not going to believe this," an enthusiastic Elaina told the group, her eyes wide. "Bull hauled Kenny in for more questioning." She waved a flash drive in the air. "*Ta da*, the Kenny interrogation." Luke reached for it, but she yanked it away and teased, "You have to be nice to me.

"I'm always nice to you."

"Buy me the buffet next time we come here?" she asked. "Here" was the dimly lit Catfish Cavern where they could sit undisturbed in a back corner for hours if they wanted.

"I'll buy you a year's worth of buffets if this helps us."

~~~

Pierre Lejune sat at the desk behind the two-way mirror in the manager's office of the Catfish Cavern. When the kids came in he followed them with dark, deep-set eyes. As they took their seats around a table in the back of the restaurant, he turned to the control panel of the "Silent Witness Surveillance" system marked "Kitchen," "Men's locker room," "Ladies locker room," "Men's restroom," "Ladies restroom," "Dining room front section," "Dining room mid-section," "Dining room back section."

The hidden video cams and microphones throughout the restaurant gave him an advantage against employee pilfering food from the kitchen, items from the locker rooms, and towels and toilet paper from the restrooms. Rumors that the boss was spying on them made honest people of them. He smiled. It was also entertaining to eavesdrop on customers. He knew who was cheating on whom, who was waiting for the results of lab tests, and who was trying to lose weight.

He hunkered over the control panel, head cocked. He flipped the switch for "Dining room back section" and put on headphones, "the better to hear you with."

~~~

Elaina handed Luke the flash drive and explained proudly, "My aunt works late at the police station so I dropped by last night under the guise of bringing her that small pizza I asked you to buy me. That got me into the back offices where I could snoop around."

"You're a genius," Luke exclaimed.

Elaina beamed. "Except for my aunt and me, the station was empty, even the jail; hasn't been anyone in that jail since forever. Spirit Mound is a small town. There's nothing for the police to do—not until the girls went missing. I glanced at my aunt's computer screen and how lucky is this? She had the Kenny interrogation audio file open!"

~~~

Pierre frowned as he eavesdropped on the kids with the Silent Witness Surveillance system. What are they up to? Something about the police station, missing girls, an interrogation?

~~~

"I had to get my aunt out of the office so I could copy the file," Elaina said. "I thought about spilling a drink so she'd go get napkins, but she'd probably make *me* get them, so I told her she had a flat tire and when she went to look I whipped out my flash drive, which I had with me, copied the file, and the deed was done, she came back in and told me her tire wasn't flat, and I said, oh, I thought it looked soft, I'm glad it isn't flat."

"Whoa, you're hyperventilating, slow down," Luke said. "Take a slow, deep breath ...."

"I took one yesterday."

"You need at least one a day," Luke said, "so take another .... good .... and another .... there, that's better ...."

"Okay," Elaina said, breathing deeply and repeating her mantra, "Deep breath, no pressure."

"Good, now go on."

"Okay, I copied the file; I could have had my butt thrown in jail if I was caught 'borrowing' evidence like that, those jail cells are so tiny and awful, and the toilet is right out in plain sight so *everyone* walking by can see you doing your thing, how embarrassing that would be, don't you think so, and I don't look good in stripes because I'm short, at least not stripes that go horizontally because they make me look shorter and heavier, stripes going up and down vertically would look better on me—"

Luke put his hand over her mouth. "Relax," he said softly in her ear, "and take *another* deep breath ... no pressure."

She complied. "I'm sorry, I just get so nervous. You're right, no pressure."

Ari had never seen anyone as melodramatic or anxious as Elaina with her hands flitting about in the air as though looking for a place to land and her eyes wide and full of whatever she was feeling at the time. It was endearing—like one might feel about a kid sister, but she didn't like Luke whispering in Elaina's ear when she wanted him to whisper in hers.

"We appreciate your sacrifice, Elaina, risking your freedom and your modesty at the police station," Luke said, and then transferred the audio file from the flash drive to iPhone. "Now let's see if we can get any speech reversals from this."

Kenny: "Karen was going out for the evening." **Hurt her**. "That was the last time I saw her, all gussied up, short skirt and all ... around seven or eight." **Her skirt off size**. "Sarah was with her." **I threat ouch.** "There was a confrontation between me and Karen. She and I used to be close, but that ended." **I and my creep sister argue. I make the girl walk, stagger**. "There was a lot of conflict between us." **The dead swim.**

"I feel like throwing up," Elaina said. Luke suggested a 10-minute break, which the girls used to congregate in the restroom.

~~~

Pierre flipped the surveillance switch, "Ladies restroom."

~~~

Ari freshened her lipstick and Elaina leaned her forehead against the mirror. Nika washed her hands and sang "Happy Birthday."

"Is it your birthday?" Jessica asked.

"No, that's how long you're supposed to wash your hands to clean them thoroughly, wash them as long as it takes you to sing one verse of Happy Birthday."

"Your talents are put to better use singing in the choir," Elaina stated. "I loved it when you sang 'Just a Closer Walk with Thee' when I went to church with you on Sunday." She sighed and rubbed her temples.

"You don't look so good, girlfriend," Nika said.

"Must be something I ate," Elaina said weakly.

"Or something you heard," Jessica stated, "like Kenny's speech reversals."

"**The dead swim**," Elaina whispered.

"It's okay to admit this scares you," Ari tried to reassure her.

Elaina nodded, but when they returned to the table she sat silently, her expression grim.

~~~

Surveillance switch: "Dining room back section."

75

~~~

Nika grew sullen as the group continued its eerie exploration.

> Kenny: "I know the way I felt about Karen." **Sin is shallow, ill water, ill water**.

Jessica wondered, "**Ill water**? Contaminated because there are bodies in it?"

> Kenny: "There was sibling rivalry when I'd come home from the Army to visit when I was younger. There was a big age difference between Karen and me, nine years" ... **There's always lumps**.

"Do you suppose Kenny hit his sister?" Jon asked. "Might that be the 'lumps' he's referring to? Or maybe she hit him. Sometimes girls hit people, too."

> Kenny: "It's a back and forth type of thing."
> **Need a sis. My wolf is sick**.

"The word **wolf** comes up quite a bit in speech reversals," Luke said. "Ari's **wolf howls** in the surf, Nika is the **angered wolf**, Kenny's **wolf is sick**. I'm not sure what it means, yet, but **wolf** might refer to a basic part of our personalities or our psyches."

> Kenny: "Karen would rely on me to take care of her and to be there for her, and then there were times she expected me to do as she told me." **I'd even ease a circuit in my arm. Might surrender. Thoughts are loosed**. "Once I started to smoke pot I didn't have to deal with much of anything."

Drugs," Jessica said softly. "He **eased a circuit** in his arm, injected something."

Elaina started to cry, "We're listening to the thoughts of a killer. People aren't supposed to do this. Maybe the unconscious mind is unconscious for a reason."

"But maybe the fact that speech reversals were discovered means we *are* meant to know about them," Luke argued.

"I don't think so," Elaina disagreed. "I've been having nightmares, like part of my brain has been activated that shouldn't have been. This isn't healthy, listening to weird backward messages. I want to do normal stuff. I want to go to the mall. I want to shop." She stood up and whimpered, "I can't do this any more. I'm going home. I like the way things used to be before we trespassed in some idiot's brain."

"Wait, Elaina, please," Luke implored and followed her to the door. Ari strained to hear what they were saying, but couldn't. Elaina was waving her hands in the air for emphasis and Luke leaned toward her, speaking softly again. Then he took her hand and they walked back to the table. "She's going to stay," he said, shaken at the thought of almost losing her. "Has anyone else had nightmares?"

"No more than usual," Todd said.

"I have insomnia," Jon said. "I used to sleep well before this mind-reading stuff."

"My dreams are better," Ari shared. "They're in color and sometimes three-dimensional."

"Do you suppose listening to speech reversals is rewiring our brains?" Nika asked.

"I don't know," Luke said. "It might take a while to realize if there are any side effects."

"Have you had bad dreams?" Ari asked him.

"Not so much bad dreams as disturbing thoughts," he answered, "like I don't know what's real anymore."

"Well, I say keep going," Jessica urged.

Kenny: "I don't think I lived with Karen for more than two months after I came back from the Army." **Pried sis from the cowboy bar. Smell whiskey**.

"The Texas Tumbleweed," Kim said. "Kenny went to the bar, but wasn't on the security camera. Maybe he snatched them up in the parking lot after they left and they put up a fight; that's why he had to pry them away."

Kenny: "After the Army I moved in with some guys, but rent got expensive, so I came back to live with my ma and Karen in the trailer park." **Hide murder**.

Luke clutched the iPhone. "Yes, Kenny, tell us where you hid the girls!"

Kenny: "I liked to drink; pot didn't do much of anything for me any more." **I need Karen, so I hurt Karen**. "I could drink and that's what I felt fine with." **A path with hell, give in**.

Bull: "So if you were to buy drugs here in town …" **Slow down. Here we go**.

Kenny: "I wouldn't buy drugs in town." **Curse those trips to Bud Miller**.

Bull: "If you were going out to buy pot around here, where would you go?" **I know who he's headed to**.

Kenny: "Probably outside town some place." **Needs a high**. "If somebody offered me a joint and I was in the right mood I might smoke it with them, but probably not. It's not my choice drug." **Hurt Karen's stomach**.

Kenny: "I've been in the vicinity of that route by the bar at least once a week since their disappearance." **Kill and remove her**. "I miss my sister." **A bum. I'm sick**.

"Oh, boy, I'm so outta here," Nika said, jumping to her feet.

"*Aw, no,*" Luke objected, "come on, we need you."

"Nope, this is the devil's work."

"Can't you be scientific instead of superstitious?" Luke lamented.

"The devil works in mysterious ways," she said.

"I thought it was God who works in mysterious ways," Luke said.

"Don't make fun of me," she snapped, on the verge of tears.

"Remember our agreement to keep this secret!" Luke reminded her.

She glared at him, "I told my minister and he doesn't like it. I've seen him twice now for counseling."

Luke winced. "You told him about us?"

"Pretty much. Well, let me know how things turn out."

Feeling angry and betrayed, he watched her leave. He glared at the group, "Does anyone else want to abandon ship?"

They shook their heads.

Luke sighed, feeling drained and miserable, and then returned with new resolve to the task at hand. "Okay, Bud Miller, who's Bud Miller? Kenny says it in reference to buying drugs."

> Bull: "You're aware that many people are beginning to wonder if you're responsible for Karen and Sarah's disappearance." **A sis drowning. He's very worried**.

"*Whoa,*" Jessica exclaimed. "Kenny used drowning reversals, **the dead swim** and **ill water**, and Bull says **a sis drowning**, like he's reading Kenny's mind."

"Here's another one that sounds like mind reading," Ari said. "When Bull asks Kenny who Kenny would go to for drugs, Kenny answers in reverse, **curse those trips to Bud Miller**, and immediately following that Bull says, **I know who he's headed to**."

Todd guessed, "Maybe when we intuitively know something about someone, we're tuning into their speech reversals."

> Bull: "Has anybody talked to you about what they think happened?" **The crime will singe you**.

> Kenny: "No. I've wondered what people think. I told a few people I thought my sister was a witch, but I never told anybody I hated her." **Shed sis. In the bush, I doubt if men are gonna clean it. I plot where to move 'em**.

> Bull: "Were you drunk the night your sister and her friend disappeared?" **I hope you're candid. I know you're scared**.

> Kenny: "(imprecise) ... at the cowboy bar." **I'm a sinner. I shot them**. "They had to (imprecise) for some reason." **We grab them a woods to die in**.

Ari noted, "He says, *I* **shot them**, and then *we* **grab them a woods to die in**, like there were more people involved."

Jessica reminded her, "Kenny said he was with his friend Joe, and the police questioned Kenny's friend Rusty of Rusty's Wreck 'n' Repair Shop."

Luke shuffled through the transcripts of the first recording. "Yeah, here Rusty says, **Their death is asleep. Ruin them. He shot 'em. I'm a sender. Are dead**. Rusty saw Kenny kill them and is subconsciously telling people what he saw, but won't consciously tell on his friend."

~~~

Pierre sat straight up in his chair. What a weird conversation those kids were having. He could barely hear the recording—a lot of it seemed garbled—but they thought that Rusty saw Kenny kill the missing girls. If that were true Rusty might get arrested for being an accomplice and that'd really screw up the lucrative partnership Pierre had with Rusty.

Pierre needed access to an automotive repair shop; his people in

Mexico hid drugs in gas tanks, airbags, and secret compartments of certain cars driven across the border into Texas. The cars were then taken to Rusty's Wreck 'n' Repair where Rusty retrieved the contraband under the guise of repairing or servicing the cars. If Rusty were implicated as an accomplice in the girls' murders, he might turn state's evidence and tell on Pierre in exchange for a lighter jail sentence.

Pierre's heart pounded, he felt faint, dizzy with worst-case scenarios; he'd lose his Catfish Cavern franchise, maybe even go to prison. Those kids had to be stopped.

~~~

Luke started the recording again, "Okay, Kenny, tell us where the girls are."

> Kenny: "I don't believe anyone would do this." **I feel lousy**. "But it seems this far into the investigation there would be more connection if it was somebody that they knew." **Have shakes. Sandy Creek is where they're missing**.

"Yes, Sandy Creek!" Luke cried, clutching the iPhone. "That's west of here on the edge of town."

"That must be the **ill water**," Elaina said. "Oh, this is chilling." She started to cry, "It's so sad. **We grab them a woods to die in**."

Luke said gently, "I know it's hard to listen to, but we're going to catch this creep."

Kenny: "So at this time I think it's (imprecise)." **I've been ill, alone, heartsick, and evil with my sis.** "I can't see my sister and Sarah just disappearing." **I drown my sin. I'm the snake.** "(imprecise) ... abduction and disappearance of people." **Don't be concerned. Sin is shallow.** "From noon Saturday I was in the trailer watching TV and cleaning up the place. I do the same thing every Saturday, lay around and watch TV." **My sis get nasty and it mess me.**

Bull: "Saturday night, after midnight, were you alone?"

Kenny: "I saw them probably about the most, forty-five minutes." **I killed the girls. I stand. I give up. I give up.**

<center>~~~</center>

Luke called Bull again from the pay phone, "We think Kenny killed the girls. He got drunk, probably did some drugs, too—he smokes grass, maybe does some hard stuff—how do I know? I know a lot of things, maybe even where the bodies are. Kenny feels real guilty. He'll be easy to crack. Bye for now," Luke said and ended the call.

"Why didn't you tell him where the bodies are?" Todd asked.

"I think we should find them ourselves. That way we'll be sure to get the reward."

"How can we see them if they're in a creek?" Elaina countered.

"**Sin is shallow**," he reminded her.

"That area west of town is mostly private property," Todd said.

"That didn't stop Kenny from going there and it shouldn't stop us."

"What if a rancher shoots us for trespassing?" Jon asked. "A property owner can do that."

"We won't be anywhere near a house," Luke said. "It'll be dark, we'll pull off the road, walk along the creek. Ari, Jessica, Elaina, Jon, you check Sandy Creek by the viaduct off Highway 733. Kim,

Todd, and I'll look farther up stream. Kenny mentioned woods and horses, so look for those. Then let's meet at the viaduct at seven o'clock to compare notes."

"I'm so nervous," Elaina exclaimed, her hands fluttering. "I hope I don't hyperventilate again." They waited for her to take a deep breath and calm herself by saying, "No pressure," and then they trooped single file out of the Catfish Cavern.

~~~

Surveillance system: off.

14. "Ill water, ill water"

In the deepening twilight Ari and Jessica both saw the bodies at the same time; over there, underwater, something gray and shadowy.

They grabbed each other's arms and inched closer, peered into the murky depths. Something—someone—was down there, just under the surface, wrapped in something like a painter's drop cloth.

"Is it—" Ari whispered.

"I think so," Jessica muttered.

"Oh, no," Ari exclaimed. "Is it both of them?"

"Yeah, huddled together," Jessica said.

Ari's eyes were opaque with the shock of seeing the soggy sheets clinging to the bodies, revealing the shape of long, slender legs, the curve of young breasts. Suddenly it looked like one of them moved and Ari thought hysterically, oh god, don't get up, are they trying to stand up? Worse than dead would be half-dead, horribly injured, and zombie-like, slimy under that soggy sheet and knowing the savage extremes to which some people go. "They moved," she cried hoarsely.

"No, they didn't," Jessica whispered fiercely. "It's just your imagination, the sheet drifting in the current."

"What's going on?" Elaina said coming up behind them, and then gasped. She stared at the water. A corner of the sheet floated loose to reveal a ghastly, bloated face. The eyes were open and milky, and long hair drifted like snarled seaweed about the head. A swollen tongue protruded from the mouth and several curious catfish swam close to the body checking it out for a potential meal.

Elaina screamed, wheezed, and started to hyperventilate, her hands flew to her face and she rubbed her cheeks, "My face is numb."

"She's having an anxiety attack," Jessica told Ari.

Elaina dropped to her knees in the grass and Jessica gently

smoothed her hair back from her forehead in an effort to calm her. "It's okay, sweetie, you'll be all right; take a deep breath."

Jon, searching a few yards away, found them huddled together, Ari's knuckles bunched against her mouth, Jessica's face pale and grim, and Elaina in the throes of an anxiety attack rocking on the ground at their feet.

He went to get Kim, Luke, and Todd while the girls stayed by the side of the creek and watched in horror as the current flowed softly over the bodies like a caress and the water continued its grim and silent digestion.

~~~

"We found the girls' bodies," Luke told Bull on his phone. "Sandy Creek near the viaduct. When you come, look for some teenagers at the side of the road."

~~~

Bull pulled off the road, parked, and approached the shaken group. "So you're the notorious Insiders," he said. "Where are the bodies?"

Luke pointed to the water and Bull crouched by the edge of the creek. The beam of his flashlight plumbed the water and found them. His shoulders slumped and he seemed profoundly disappointed. There was nothing he could do for them now. He couldn't negotiate or fight for them. The girls were dead and it happened in his town.

He called for an ambulance and told the driver where to come, "But no rush; they're dead." Then he walked around the area, moved the weeds with his toe, and scribbled a few notes on a pad of paper.

Luke stood tall, his jaw tight; brave. Ari wanted to comfort him, but didn't know how, and needed consoling herself. Against the windswept hills he looked small and vulnerable. She figured he must be in shock from seeing the bodies. Stay strong, Luke, please, for the rest of us.

Bull's deputy, Hank Cooper, and the ambulance pulled up one after the other. The paramedics, wearing air filters to protect them against the pungent, nauseating smell of decaying flesh dragged

85

them from the creek. The catfish swam away.

Ari noticed the girls were wearing boots made for dance floors—so out of place in a creek.

Hank wiped the mud off the girls' chalk-white faces. "It's them," he grimaced.

The paramedics loaded the sheet with its soggy cargo onto stretchers and slid the girls' bodies into the back of the ambulance, but not before Ari got a whiff: the sharp smell of putrid flesh pierced her defenses and stung the back of her throat. She stepped back and gagged. In death, Karen and Sarah asserted themselves one last time, their gruesome condition a silent, sad request: avenge us.

After the ambulance drove off and Hank left to return to the police station, Bull turned to the group. "I want your names, phone numbers, and addresses, and then I want you to meet me at the station for questioning. I'll be there as soon as I secure things here." He took a large roll of yellow crime-scene tape out of the police car and tossed it on the ground by the creek.

As they gave him their names, numbers, and addresses, the rising wind clawed at their hair and clothes and a dark cloud rose like a bruise against the glare of the setting sun. And some distance away, a white van pulled up and parked with a man in it who had deep-set, dark colored eyes. Stenciled on the side of the van: **Catfish Cavern**.

15. Unnerved

Hank had the group sit in the waiting room at the police station and led Luke past the front desk, down a long hall, and out of sight. Ari was terrified. Are the police going to torture him? She rocked back and forth and whispered frantically, "Don't hurt him, *don't hurt him*!"

"He'll be okay," Jessica tried to reassure her.

"What if it's like in Iran?" Ari said in a small voice.

"I'm sure he'll be okay."

Hank ushered Luke into a back office where Bull nodded for him to sit. "How'd you know where the bodies were?"

"*Ummm*, we got a recording of the, *ah*, I mean a copy of, *ahum*—" He was afraid to admit that they had a copy of the interrogation.

"Quit stammering. Tell me what happened."

Luke cleared his throat to try to preempt any incriminating speech reversals of his own. He knew that every time he spoke, his unconscious mind added commentary of its own in the form of speech reversals—an echo he couldn't hear. He wanted to look over his shoulder to see who—or what—was following him, but he knew it'd just be himself. He spoke hesitantly like someone who hears his own voice coming back to him—delayed—over a phone with a bad connection. What if he told on Elaina—in reverse—about how she "borrowed" the audio file? What if Bull sensed what he was thinking?

"I'll demonstrate," Luke said and played the TV broadcast and corresponding speech reversals. Bull looked amazed, and then when he heard his own reversal, **I feel nasty weather**, the expression on his face disappeared like a stream vanishing down a sinkhole.

Luke sympathized, "When I heard my reversals for the first time I was shocked, too." Then he played highlights from the Kenny interrogation audio file—praying that Bull would be too fascinated with the reversals to ask how Luke got the file—and pointed out, "Kenny's final speech reversal is so incriminating, **I killed the girls. I stand. I give up. I give up.**"

Bull slumped in his chair. Luke said, "I know this is a lot to absorb." Bull's silence made him nervous, but he forged ahead. "Some of these other reversals might be helpful, too, like **curse those trips to Bud Miller**, which we found on Kenny's forward dialogue, 'I wouldn't buy drugs here in town.' Bud Miller might be a drug dealer."

Bull swallowed noticeably. "How'd you get ahold of the interrogation—"

"And how about this," Luke interrupted, "Sounds like Kenny does hard drugs, **I'd even ease a circuit in my arm**. You might be able to trace the trail of reversals to a drug dealer."

Luke couldn't gauge Bull's reaction. "I know this is a lot to think about, so I'll leave a copy of the transcript with you and come back tomorrow for the reward. Okay?"

Bull just grunted, "*Uh*," so Luke coached him, "I imagine you have more questions for Kenny. May I suggest that you weave a few of his *own* speech reversals into the questions you ask him and see what happens, just to experiment?"

Bull nodded slowly, "Sure."

Luke stood up. "Should I have the others come in? You can get their take on this?"

Bull shook his head and said flatly, "No. I've heard enough."

~~~

"Did you talk to Kenny?" Luke wanted to know the next day when he, Ari, and Elaina returned to the police station.

"Yeah, I picked him up for more questioning," Bull said. "He didn't know we found the girls."

"Did you feed him any of his own reversals?" Luke asked.

"Not until I got tired of how unresponsive he was, the murdering son-of-a—" Bull regained his composure and continued,

"So I used his reversals like you suggested. I told him that I knew he **needed a sis**, and that his **wolf was sick**."

"What'd he say?"

"He turned white as sheet, and I asked him how **shallow his sin was**, and he started to shake and tilted sideways in the chair like he was going to faint, and then I demanded to know why the **water was ill**."

"What'd he do?"

"He threw up on the floor and confessed."

~~~

"So when do we get the reward?" Luke asked.

"It'll take a couple weeks to clear with the people who put up the money—Sarah's family," Bull told him. "Karen didn't have any family to speak of, other than Kenny and you know how that turned out."

"Let's call the newspaper with the story," Elaina said.

"No," Bull responded sharply, "don't go to the media. It wouldn't look good."

"What will you tell Sarah's family," Ari asked, "when they want to know how the case was solved?"

"I'll tell them they don't need to know all the details. It should be enough that we caught the guy," Bull said.

"You can make out the check to The Insiders," Luke told him. "I opened a bank account specifically for the group so we can work on more cases and get more rewards."

"If people find out I used something as airy-fairy as this to solve a case I'd be the laughing stock of the town," Bull fretted. "People would lose all faith in me."

"But it solved the murder," Ari objected. "If more people know about speech reversals more people can be helped."

Bull shook his head, "No, it's fringe science at best. We took so much flack for bringing in a psychic on one case: people complained, religious fanatics denounced us as devil worshipers, and the police chief at the time had to resign."

"Did the psychic solve the case?" Elaina asked.

"She gave us a decent lead," Bull admitted, "but no, she didn't solve it."

"This is different," Ari persisted. "We *did* solve the case. We even found the bodies."

"Just don't discuss it with anyone!" Bull ordered.

Silenced, they were bewildered. Bull was totally unappreciative, but as they were leaving, he softened. "Listen, maybe I could use you as consultants on cases; my secret weapon. I just don't want anyone to know how the case was solved, yet. I'm a little unnerved by all this."

16. The Time Machine

Luke sat at the computer in his bedroom. His hair was disheveled and he hadn't changed clothes in three days. A sandwich, with one bite taken out of it, sat ignored and growing stale on a plate while he searched his database looking for historical recordings that he could upload and reverse. Is it possible to tell when the speech reversal phenomena started, to trace it back to the beginning? He went back more than four decades:

> A reporter's live commentary of the President Kennedy assassination (November 22, 1963): **He's shot bad. Hold it. Try and look up**.

> Neil Armstrong, first man to walk on the moon (July 20, 1969): **Man will space walk**.

> Former President Bush revealing the code word for the Persian Gulf War while the operation was still referred to as "Desert Shield," before it became Desert Storm (1990): **Simone in the sands**. Note: "Simoon" is an Arabic word for a desert storm.

> Prisoners of war during Desert Storm (1991): **Warn my home. You hurt. Do you know this hell?**

He pulled up another file: August 17, 1980, a nine-week old baby disappeared while her family was camping near Ayers Rock, a popular tourist spot in Australia. The parents claimed that a wild dog, a dingo, took the baby. Authorities searched the area and found no evidence of that. The baby's mother was charged with murder and sentenced to life in prison. Luke studied her first interview with the police.

"I yelled at the dog and I thought that's the baby's cry, he's disturbed her." **Help us. God the warrior**.

"I said the dingo's got my baby and I was running, as I said this, around the car and there was the dingo standing at the back of the car." **I was running. I needed the wind**. "I chased it and there was nothing. It was all shadows and I just, *er*, Michael ran from the barbecue straight into the dark and I called out has anyone got a flashlight?" **Slip on our shoes. I needed shoes**.

In 1986, authorities confirmed she told the truth when they found the baby's bloody clothing and concluded that a canine had carried it off. She was cleared of all charges and released, but only after she spent six years in prison.

Luke felt such compassion for the desperate mother who called for the speed, the power, and the strength of the wind to help her save her baby. Her reversals brought a depth to her suffering and intensity to her anguish that media interviews couldn't begin to reveal—in the forward speech.

How many innocent people are languishing in prison right now, how many guilty were freed, how many innocent executed? How many more will die before speech reversals can be proven scientifically and accepted? He lost his appetite. He slipped the sandwich into the wastebasket. He had to focus on one case at a time and forget everyone who was needlessly lost throughout history. What was done was done. He had to choose which cases to study and which to ignore no matter how deserving they all were.

He moved up through the years and found speech reversals on parents suspected in the disappearance of children, on celebrities, on conspiracy theories of every kind, and on presidential candidates.

Reversal analysis isn't for the squeamish, the impatient, or those who want quick results. It's hard, demanding work. He sipped water from a tall glass and continued to listen to history in reverse and began to understand so many things in a new light. Besides being a truth detector, speech reversals were also a time machine that enabled him to understand history from a totally different perspective.

He felt dizzy with despair and a deeper, nagging worry: do I have the right to involve my friends in this? It took a toll on Nika and Elaina is ready to crack. So many things to consider: possibilities, implications, and the scorn or fanaticism of others. He wanted to escape from all the responsibility he created for himself. He looked forward to—no, *craved*—the soothing, altered state that listening to reversals induced in him. Even the gibberish was calming; and in the garden of that gibberish reversals blossomed like strange flowers, poetry and profanity, need and desire, voices of children calling to each other across the crowded playgrounds of life.

I am perfume / I see the Garden / Who will love me / It's the Whirlwind, not I / I feel awed / The Wolf speaks with power, there is no other one / Now for the magician / I share your face

When his mother knocked on the door and he didn't answer she peeked in. "You okay?" she asked, and glanced at his computer screen—no doubt checking to make sure he wasn't on a porn site.

He looked up with glazed eyes that reflected how overwhelmed he felt and how exhausted he was becoming.

"If something were wrong, you'd tell me, wouldn't you?" she asked.

He nodded, at a loss for words.

17. The Interrogation

Ari's mother Maryam began her interrogation with a statement, "I picked up Chinese food and your father's working late so it'll just be us for dinner." She set cartons on the table and took out plates, bowls, and silverware. "Now tell me about your friends and your project."

Ari took some moo-shu chicken and fried rice. "It's something we might be able to use for extracurricular credit when school starts in the fall."

Maryam smiled. "We did the right thing coming to America. In Iran Bahá'ís girls are banned from higher education. If we hadn't left Iran, you'd be at home preparing for your 'real' life as a wife instead of working on your school project. Now tell me about it."

"It's a voice-analysis technique. We're trying to figure out how to measure stress levels in people's voices. Everyday modern stress, the stress of living."

"Wonton soup?"

"I don't think soup causes stress," Ari joked, "I hear that a bowl of hearty soup helps alleviate it. "No soup, I'm tired. I just want to go to bed."

"It's 7:15. Are you sick? Do you have a fever?" She brushed back her daughter's dark curls and felt her forehead. "*Hmmm,* you feel cool, no fever."

"A couple girls from school were murdered." She stopped short of saying, I found the bodies and they were slimy and smelled and I feel sick just thinking about it.

"I'm sorry; friends of yours?"

"No, but one was my age." She remembered last night's terrifying dream: the girls, wrapped in sheets, stood up in the stream, reached out to her, and pleaded "Don't leave us here."

"Do they know who did it?"

"The half brother of one of the girls."

"That's a relief that they got him. We don't want a weirdo running around town." She waited for Ari to agree, but when she didn't, she asked gently, "Do you want a fortune cookie, at least?"

"Yeah." Ari opened it and read, "You are the mast of every situation." She smiled, "I like it. A mast on a ship supports the sails and rigging. Without it, the ship can't go anywhere."

"I think it means that you're the *master* of every situation," Maryam countered. "Mine says, 'You deserve some peace and quiet.'"

Ari laughed. "I could use some peace and quiet myself right about now."

18. The Work of the Devil

"What does *that* mean?" Elaina asked when Nika met her in line at the movie theater wearing a t-shirt with the words, "I'm a Hypocrite" printed on the front.

"They sell these at church. It means that if we *say* we believe what the Bible teaches, but *act* differently, we're hypocrites."

The minister, Pastor Ted, at the mega-church Nika attended was known for confrontational sermons and provocative advertising. It drew people in by the thousands. The parking lot filled up so quickly on Sundays that the church had remote parking lots and shuttles to bring people to the front door.

"Why call yourself a hypocrite?" Elaina asked. "You're honest, too, and tell the truth, so you're a truth-sayer. You could wear that on your shirt."

"You're missing the point."

"I guess so," Elaina admitted as they bought their movie tickets. "Does the Bible talk about speech reversals?"

"Not exactly."

Elaina paid for a bucket of popcorn at the snack concession. "Luke says that speech reversals are something we all do naturally; just another way to communicate."

Nika dug sullenly into her bucket of popcorn and followed Elaina into the dimly lit theater. As they took their seats Nika said, "Pastor Ted says they're the work of the devil and he's very alarmed."

"Luke didn't want us to tell anyone about speech reversals."

"Luke has you wound around his little finger. You'd do anything for him, wouldn't you?"

"I do like him," Elaina admitted, flustered. "Who wouldn't?"

"You even analyze speech reversals because Luke asks you to. Pastor Ted says that Satan is working *through* Luke through his curiosity. Satan wants people to do things backwards like listen to music backwards and walk and talk backwards."

"Are you doing the devil's work if you put your car in reverse to back out of the garage?"

"Don't be ridiculous."

"But I don't get it," Elaina said, confused, "What's wrong with doing things backwards? It's just another direction. Are cars and airplanes unnatural? God gave us legs and feet, not wheels or wings, so maybe God wanted us to walk instead of drive or fly."

Nika mumbled through a mouthful of popcorn, "*Aye yie yie*, you're testing my patience. God gave us the creativity to invent cars and airplanes."

"Then maybe he gave us the creativity to discover and work with speech reversals."

"Pastor Ted has been to seminary. He's a Bible scholar and I believe him. Listening to speech reversals is the work of the devil. End of argument."

The lights in the theater went out. It would take a while for their eyes to adjust to the dark.

19. Hooking Up

"When we were telling our secrets at the first meeting, you didn't say anything," Todd reminded Jon as they set up their speech-reversal equipment on Jon's screened-in back porch. "Is there something you didn't tell us? It'll come out sooner or later if we keep studying speech reversals."

Jon thought a moment and then half whispered, "Okay, just between us, I hooked up with Jim Bob's girlfriend after the homecoming game, in the equipment shed."

Todd gasped, delighted, "You *didn't*. Jim Bob, captain of the football team, you got with his girlfriend?" He beamed.

"That's okay with you? I thought you wouldn't like to hear about someone hooking up with a girl."

"Because I'm gay?" He laughed. "No, it's always fun when people connect. I'm happy for you."

"Well, it was stupid. Jim Bob would kill me."

"I won't tell. You're keeping *my* secret. He'd kill us both, a 'nerd' and a 'fag,' and probably punch out his girlfriend, too."

"It must be terrible for Jim Bob to feel that it's *his* responsibility to make everyone behave," Jon said.

"Was it your first time?"

"Sort of."

"Was it hers?"

"I don't think so. She seemed to know what she was doing."

"So how was she?"

"What do you care?"

"I dunno. It'd be fun to know."

He smiled, remembering, "She was great."

"But if it was 'sort of' your first time, you don't have anything to compare it to."

"It was fantastic, so shut up."

"Are you going to do it again?"

"As often as I can with anyone who wants to, *sheesh*. So do your parents know you're gay?"

"Way to go; change the subject. They suspect it. Mom wants us to go to family counseling, 'just for a tune-up,' she says, quick to say that 'our family is fine, really, really fine, the family dynamic works very, very, *very* well'—and she wants to make sure it stays that way. She just wants to get *me* in front of a shrink. We go in with the excuse that we're there for *family* counseling, but *I'm* the one they want psychoanalyzed."

"Maybe she just wants to encourage you to come out. Maybe she's being supportive."

"No, I've seen the disapproving looks she gives people who are gay, I hear her comments. She wants to 'cure' me; but this isn't a cold or the flu. It's like having brown eyes or blue eyes or being right handed. It's the way I am." He was growing agitated, "I'd like to see everyone who's straight be told they have to become gay starting tomorrow. They'd think that was the most outrageous thing they ever heard, but they expect *me* to switch."

"Do you have a boyfriend?"

"There's someone at Dalton High. We kid around at track meets, but haven't 'connected' in that way, yet."

"What makes him special?"

"He's sexy and fun. Why do you like Jim Bob's girlfriend?"

"She's sexy and fun," Jon smiled, and then his eyes narrowed, nervous, "You don't have the hots for anyone in *our* group, do you?"

"Don't flatter yourself."

"Maybe I am a little paranoid."

"You mean homophobic."

He shrugged. "Are you going to tell your parents?"

"I suppose eventually, but once I say it I can't take it back, and they might disown me." He smiled sadly. "Someone once said 'Be yourself; everyone else is already taken.' I like that."

"I think you're doing a *great* job being yourself. Do you think anyone in our group has hooked up?"

"The most likely are Luke and Ari," Todd guessed. "I see how they look at each other, but then again, Ari seems real shy and reserved, so I don't know. Jessica is mysterious; who knows what she does outside the group. Kim's busy with Karate, Elaina's too young, and I don't think Nika's religion would let her."

"I suppose if we wait long enough, our speech reversals will tell on all of us," Jon concluded. "People aren't going to be able to get away with anything anymore."

20. At the Dojo

Kim looked forward to running laps to warm up at the dojo, the mixed-martial-arts studio that his parents owned. The first 30 laps around the large room were easy; the next 20 laps, more challenging, but Kim didn't break a sweat.

The following 30 pushups were painful. Kim's friend Raymond, in his first year of college, had the nerves in his hands severed so he could do pushups on his knuckles without feeling the pain; knuckles don't have any fat to cushion them. Raymond's knuckles were large and calloused. Kim examined his own knuckles; enlarged and bruised, but he couldn't imagine having the nerves cut. He tried to think of the "pain" as "an interesting sensation" while he counted: 1 … 2 … 3 … all the way to 30.

Next came sit-ups; 30 of those, too. Raymond was a fanatic for sit-ups and had the abs to prove it. He came to the studio early to do them; one day he did 1,003 sit-ups in 23 minutes; "44.9 average per minute," he announced proudly.

After the intense warm up the students did a series of *katas*, movements designed to improve their balance and help them become proficient in the art.

Kim looked forward to spending time at the dojo. His parents designed the entry to be a perfect transition from the hectic outside world to an inner world of strength and self-knowledge. They followed Feng Shui principles, the ancient Chinese art of arranging one's surroundings to attract positive life energy, or "chi," so it flows smoothly within a room and within the body. People are affected—for better or worse—by their surroundings. The soft music, plants, and standing waterfall in the corner calmed Kim. He'd take a few deep breaths to clear his head, and then go into the locker room to change into his "gi," his Karate uniform made of heavy durable canvas; it made a wonderful, satisfying "snapping" sound when he punched and kicked.

Kim had a lot of adrenaline to work off. Finding Karen and Sarah's bodies in the creek was getting to him; he was easily distracted, like being in a fog. Exercise helped to clear his head.

The last thing they did in class was to pair off and free fight to practice what they learned. They had to stop kicks and punches an inch from their partners' bodies so they didn't injure them. If someone got too rough, the instructor had everyone stop, take a deep breath, and continue. Kim didn't mind being paired with Raymond because what Raymond had in strength and stamina, Kim made up for in flexibility and agility; the person who masters the most moves wins the fight. Kim knew how to kill a man with the palm of his hand, escape a chokehold, and break the hold if someone grabbed him from behind. Confidence came easy for him.

After the workout Kim's father spoke with him privately. "It's going to take you twice as long as the other students to master the skills."

"Why?" Kim asked, surprised.

"A lot of your attention is on how well Raymond is doing."

"He's very good. I admire his dedication."

His father smiled, "I sense that you're wrestling with your competitive nature. When you look at how well others are doing, your attention wanders; you lose the excellence of who you are."

Kim nodded his understanding and then did a few more katas. The dojo gave him the opportunity to practice and train in the art of living. Of all The Insiders he had the most patience and focus to work with speech-reversal analysis. They were all a bunch of nerves, emotions, reservations, and worries.

21. Walking the Dogs

At twilight Jessica walked along the horse trail by the lake accompanied by the neighbors' dogs who were hysterical with joy to spend time with her and go down to the water.

Katie and Scout were spaniels from the same litter, Harley was a big golden retriever, Tanner, a gangly short hair pointer with big feet, and Luna, a huge black lab puppy. Katie was the smartest, Harley the goofiest, and Luna the most rambunctious. Tanner was sweet and loving. He smiled whenever he saw Jessica. His upper lip curled back over his teeth and he wagged his entire body—starting with his nose all the way down to the tip of his long, tapered tail— like the "wave" that people do in sports stadiums.

Scout was notorious for crashing parties in the neighborhood. He was drawn to music and people's voices. Someone would let him into the house and he'd flop down in the middle of the floor like he lived there and soak up all the good party vibes.

The dogs didn't go to the lake by themselves without a human along. They seemed to understand that wild things lived down there: rattlesnakes, water moccasins, copperheads, coyotes, foxes, bobcats, wild boar, and a rumored mountain lion. They didn't mind the shy deer, illusive raccoons, possums, armadillos, and rabbits, nor did they mind an occasional skunk, unless they got sprayed, but they fully respected and avoided the venomous and dangerous animals. There was a big dog, Boudreaux, who had his throat torn out. "A wolf," the veterinarian thought, although the Army Corps of Engineers, who managed the area around the lake, said there hadn't been any wolves in Texas since the early 1900s. Jessica wasn't so sure. She thought she saw one once.

Just as the dogs wouldn't walk by the lake without a human, Jessica wouldn't go down there without the dogs. It was too remote. Karen and Sarah's murders were still fresh in her mind. She watched the dogs spinning and dancing and jumping about her, and laughed, "Who's protecting whom?"

The dogs loved it by the lake and welcomed any opportunity to go for a walk. They came over every evening because Jessica showed them a good time even though they ran ahead of her on the path, out of sight, but they doubled back frequently to make sure she was still coming. She was the alpha dog that couldn't keep up.

Katie and Tanner rolled in a rotting carp on the shore, a skunk sprayed Scout, and Tanner cut his tail on a thorn, but wagged it anyway, seemingly oblivious to the wound. Harley ate horse poop he found on the trail.

All the dogs swam in the lake, and then ventured into the underbrush to explore, sniff around, and eat grass. How they managed to avoid the snakes, spiders, and scorpions every time they went for a walk, Jessica would never know.

Coming up the steep hill through the meadow to her house, she felt the familiar wheeze of asthma that came on whenever she overexerted herself in warm, muggy weather. Her asthma had never been bad enough, at least not yet, to warrant medical attention. It was more a warning to be careful and respect her limitations. Maybe that's one of the reasons she valued thinking so much. She could go anywhere in her mind, do anything in her imagination, and it wouldn't make her sneeze or wheeze.

The dogs charged past her up the hill to wait at the top. They were panting, tails wagging, tongues lolling out, grinning. They were a smelly, winded, wounded, muddied, bloodied, soggy pack. It had been an absolutely glorious walk.

Jessica pulled up a lawn chair and the dogs settled around her. "I don't know, kids," she told them, "this Insiders work is a strange turn of events. I like everyone, though. Luke's so nice, and Elaina, too. She's younger than the rest of us, and acts it. I'm the only one who has graduated so far. Jon and Luke will be seniors in high school in the fall."

Tanner listened intently while Scout dozed and Harley licked himself in inappropriate places. Luna, who had Attention Deficit Disorder, already left the yard in search of something else to do.

"Ari is beautiful," Jessica told the dogs, "clear, olive skin. Kids would kill for a complexion like that. She's hard to figure out, though. Very smart—speaks perfect English even though it's her second language—but she doesn't talk about her life in Iran. Oh, and Todd. What can I say about him?"

Tanner's ears perked up.

"His speech reversal said he's gay, although he didn't admit it. Let's see, Jon loves astronomy, Kim's into Karate, and Luke's really cute, a leader, I think, although more easy-going than charismatic. And Nika; she's pretty, but judgmental, real concerned about doing what's right—according to *her* values, not ours necessarily. I think she wants to be the conscience of the group, to tell us what's right and wrong, moral and immoral. Do you know what I mean?" Tanner woofed and she told him, "Like you value rolling in horse poop and chasing skunks and drinking stagnant pond water. It's not what I like to do, but you like it and that's fine with me. I don't judge you for it."

Tanner whined.

"What? You want to know if I'm going to tell my parents that I found the girls' bodies?" Tanner wagged his tail. She sighed. "I don't think so. How would I explain? Oh, by the way, Mom and Dad, I found a couple dead bodies while I was on the edge of town looking for them because I knew they'd be there. How'd I know where to look? A mind-reading machine told me. A mind-reading machine; imagine that."

A Whippoorwill called in the deep woods and the dogs raised their noses to the wind, sensing things in the dark that Jessica couldn't begin to perceive. She closed her eyes. Her thoughts drifted and the stars came out.

22. Gone

"Have we got a recording for you!"

"Elaina?" Luke asked.

"Yeah, and Kim's here, too. We have a recording you are *not* going to believe. No way I can tell you on the phone."

"Send it to me."

"No, I've got to see you. I'll bring it on a flash drive; it's more secure that way—an email could be traced. Meet me at Piggly Wiggly on Highway 733 in two hours—by the dairy case, 9 p.m. sharp. Bye."

Luke called Ari and asked her to meet them, too. He wanted her company.

~~~

Ari paced up and down the dairy aisle. She met Luke on time, but no Elaina or Kim. Luke went to look for them on his Harley and she stayed behind in case they showed up. She tried to call them—no answer. She bought a bottle of sparkling mineral water and went outside to wait. Country Western music from The Texas Tumbleweed, a couple blocks away, filled the humid night. The Tumbleweed was the last place Karen and Sarah were seen alive. It sounded like such a fun place. But then the music changed moods, and the plaintive, melancholy "You Were Always on my Mind" began about a guy who didn't tell his girl often enough that he loved her and maybe didn't treat her as well as he should have, but she was always on his mind.

The rumble of the Harley announced Luke's arrival as he pulled up, "Get on. I found them and it's bad, *real* bad."

They headed out of town. Ari usually loved the flat stretches of 733 as it ran past streams, vast meadows, and ranchlands. Out here on a clear night you could see galaxies without a telescope—misty fingerprints in the heavens; no wonder Jon was intrigued by the stars. But tonight she didn't appreciate the scenery or the stars. She was wondering if Luke communicated something in reverse when he said, "It's bad, *real* bad." She pressed her cheek against his leather jacket and fought her fear.

The road held the heat of the day and filled her nostrils with the smell of hot, dry asphalt. The Harley's tires hummed. Let's just keep going all the way to Houston or Corpus Christi, we can walk on the beach, collect shells, find a pier with a little restaurant and eat seafood—shrimp, scallops, and fresh crab with drawn butter. Let's ride far away from where we are.

Her heart sank; there ahead, two ambulances on the dark shoulder of the road and the garish flashing red and blue lights of Bull's police cruiser—a coyote tail attached to the antenna flapped in the wind. Kim's car had gone off the road and plowed through the wildflowers into a grain silo. He was strapped on a gurney—a paramedic fitting him with a neck brace. They'd already slid the other gurney with Elaina on it into one of the ambulances.

Luke rushed to Kim's side. "Hey, buddy, it's me, Luke."

"He can't hear you," Bull said flatly, "he's unconscious. And the other one is gone."

"Gone?" Luke exclaimed and Ari let out a strangled cry, knowing exactly what he meant.

"She's dead," Bull stated.

Ari wanted to demand that Bull back what he said. She had the crazy thought that if Bull hadn't said it, Elaina would still be here; by saying that she died, he made it true.

"Stupid kids were drag racing. The other driver must have lost control and hit them."

Luke and Ari rushed to Kim's side; he was stirring, mumbling. His nose was broken, face swelling. Luke gripped his hand as though he might escape. "Stay with us, buddy."

"They weren't wearing seatbelts," Bull said. "*Always* wear seatbelts!"

Luke whispered in Kim's ear, "Where's the flash drive Elaina was bringing us?" Kim groaned, his eyelids fluttered. "Who were you racing?" Luke demanded.

"Nika."

Luke was astonished. "Was Nika driving the other car?"

Kim lapsed back into unconsciousness as the paramedic pried his hand from Luke's grip and slid the gurney into one of the ambulances, slammed the door, jumped into the front seat, and sped off. The ambulance carrying Elaina followed.

Luke whispered to Ari, "Keep Bull occupied while I look for the flash drive."

She burst out crying, took a couple steps toward Bull, and collapsed. He caught her on her way to the ground. He looked flustered. "Hey, it's okay," he told her.

"No, it's not," she cried. "My friend is dead." Just hearing the words made it even more unbearable and she began to sob uncontrollably. She hung on Bull's arm, and every time he tried to turn around to talk to Luke, she clutched him tighter.

"My friends, my friends," she sobbed.

"*Aw*, your nose is running," Bull said. "Don't you have a tissue?"

She sniffed loudly, repeatedly, and rubbed away her hot tears, "No I don't."

"Well I don't carry any with me."

She pressed her face to his sleeve and took big gulps of air, shaking uncontrollably.

"Hey, come here and take care of your girlfriend," he ordered Luke. "What are you doing in that car? Get out of the car! It's a crime scene."

"I'm looking for a tissue for her," Luke said, searching the glove box one last time. He already rifled through Elaina's purse.

"I'm going to have to arrest you for not following police orders."

Luke jumped out of the car. "Okay, I've got her," he said, taking Ari's arm and pulling her to him.

Bull brushed himself off. Comforting a sobbing, hysterical teenager wasn't in his skill set or job description. "You kids go home now." He headed toward his patrol car.

"Good job," Luke told Ari.

"I wasn't acting," she said miserably. "Did you find the flash drive?"

"No. Let's go to the hospital and see if Kim has it." But when they got there the nurses told them that they hadn't found a flash drive on either of their friends, and Kim was in a coma.

~~~

Ari curled into herself on a chair in the hospital corridor and cried despondently. Luke slipped an arm around her. "I'll take you back to your car." On the way he stopped the motorcycle at the side of a quiet country road. They got off to look at the moon, full and orange and silent. It'd been up there in place probably since the creation of the solar system, ancient and far removed from the life and death drama of people's lives.

Elaina had been a human being with a history, experiences, a family, litanies of belief, stories, a repertoire of feelings, people she loved, people who loved her, and now she was gone, gone, gone, and only the moon remained. Ari felt her absence—hollow and empty—to the core of her being. There was one less heartbeat in the world. She leaned against a tree and sobbed, "Elaina, where are you? I want to go where you are!"

23. Speeding?

"I didn't know you knew about cars," Luke told Jon at the accident site as he handed Jon a copy of the accident report he picked up at the police station. "I thought you were all about astronomy."

"Liking stars doesn't preclude me liking cars," Jon smiled. "My brother's a race car driver. I help out in the pit stop at the Lone Star Motor Speedway on race weekends. It helps me get out of my intellect and into my instinct. A car usually pits two or three times during a race for refueling, mechanical adjustments, new tires. We have to analyze problems in a split second, fix them, and get the car back in the race. A race can be won or lost in a matter of seconds. It's quite a change of pace from photographing stars. Last weekend it took me five-and-a-half-hours to record a trail of stars."

Luke marveled at the difference in timing between the two activities and admired Jon's ability to do each well. "I can see you're the best one to analyze the accident report. Why didn't Bull mention another car? And where is it now? Were Kim and Elaina speeding?"

Jon adjusted his glasses, glanced at the accident report and then slipped it into the pocket of his backpack. "Since Kim's in a coma and can't tell us, let's see if the facts add up."

He crouched down to study the skid marks on the pavement, then ambled down the road and examined the weeds on the shoulder. "*Hmmm,*" he said, frowning at the furrow Kim's car plowed into the ditch. "The report said that both Kim and Elaina were found outside the car and weren't wearing seatbelts. It also said it couldn't be determined who was driving." He sighed. "Kim was driving *and* wearing a seatbelt."

"How do you know?"

"When you asked me to look into this, I talked to the doctor on duty the night they were taken to the emergency room. He said Kim had an elongated bruise on his left shoulder, which indicated he was wearing a seatbelt and driving."

"Did Elaina have a bruise?" Luke asked.

"Not on her shoulder, so she probably wasn't wearing a seatbelt and was the only one of the two of them thrown from the car. Kim undid his seatbelt and got out, trying to get to her."

"But that's a minor point." Luke asked. "What does that have to do with anything?"

"It's significant in that Bull overlooked something so obvious."

"It sounds like you don't think much of the accident report."

"Let's wait until we have a look at the car," Jon said. "Did you say it's at Rusty's Wreck 'n' Repair?"

"Yeah," Luke said, "but Rusty won't be there. The police have been looking for him to question him in connection with Karen and Sarah's murders, but can't find him."

~~~

Rusty's Wreck 'n' Repair was a cavernous garage that smelled of grease and motor oil. Cars sat around in various stages of repair, their parts either hanging out or strewn across the floor. A mechanic led them to Kim's wrecked car in the back. "Take all the time you need," he told them. "I can't hang around, though. We're short-handed today."

"Rusty not here?" Luke asked, knowing the answer.

"Nope. He called from Louisiana. Said he was headed to New Orleans for some cool jazz and a hot date," the mechanic smiled, then returned to the car on which he was working.

"Yeah, right," Luke whispered to Jon. "He's probably going in the opposite direction."

"Too bad we don't have a recording of Rusty," Jon said and ran his hand slowly down one side of the wrecked car.

"Bull said they were speeding," Luke said, "but Kim was too smart to endanger their lives, and besides, Elaina wouldn't let him. Speeding would give her an anxiety attack."

Jon nodded and then extracted a light from his backpack,

yanked open the bent door on the driver's side, and disappeared into the interior. When he popped back out, he confirmed, "Bull was right. They were speeding, doing 89 miles an hour in a 65-mile-an-hour zone." He answered Luke's disbelieving look with an explanation. "This is a vintage Chrysler. On old cars like this, speedometer needles have a phosphorescent coating that glows. The coating can stick to the speedometer cover in a high-speed crash and indicate the speed the car was traveling at impact. Look." He shone a light on the dashboard. "This black light illuminates the phosphorescent coating. See the faint glow on the glass?"

"It does say 89—almost 90 miles an hour—but Kim wasn't reckless."

"Did Bull tell you the two cars collided?" Jon asked.

"Yeah."

"I don't think so. This car was sideswiped. See the groove along the side? And look at this." He passed Luke a magnifying glass. Tiny flecks of white paint sparkled in the grove. "Bull told you there was a second vehicle, but didn't mention it in his report."

"Because he felt guilty for not apprehending the other driver?" Luke speculated.

"I don't know. If Kim and Elaina were drag racing someone, they probably would have been racing someone from school. But their car was sideswiped. That points to a more experienced driver. It takes a lot of skill to sideswipe another vehicle and not lose control of your own."

"It's like Bull is hiding something," Luke said, baffled.

"It could just be sloppy police work."

"But what about the flash drive Elaina was bringing us?" Luke asked. "What was on it and where is it? It wasn't in the car or in her purse or on Kim at the hospital. It disappeared."

24. In the ICU

The highly polished floor of the hospital hallway reflected the overhead lights and reinforced the sterile, antiseptic feeling of the place. Luke, Ari, Todd, Jon, and Jessica walked in a tight group toward a small waiting room reserved for friends and families of patients in the Intensive Care Unit.

"I'm Dr. Owen, please have a seat. Your friend has a closed-head, traumatic brain injury; it's not evident from the outside, except for cuts and bruising. He's comatose. You can go in one at a time for two minutes each. There's some evidence that coma patients can hear what people say to them, so don't say anything that might upset him, and whatever you do, don't mention that his friend died."

"Will he recover?" Ari asked hopefully.

"It's too early to tell. There's some swelling in the brain, but we have state-of-the art equipment. He's in good hands. Okay, who wants to go in first? I'll go with you."

Luke approached Kim tentatively, "I'm so sorry, man. We're here for you." He leaned closer, whispered, "Where's the flash drive?"

"*Whoa*," Dr. Owen exclaimed. "I don't know what that means, but I'm pretty sure he can't answer." He ushered Luke out the door and motioned for Ari to come in.

She approached Kim hesitantly. "We're praying for you, Kim. Please get well soon."

Jon came in next, "Hey, Kim, they know what they're doing here. They have *tons* of diagnostic equipment. When you feel better you can Feng Shui this place. I mean, is *that* the best position for an EEG monitor, and shouldn't the head of the bed face north?"

"Everything's in the best position for what it's used for," Dr. Owen smiled. "Next."

Todd simply said "Hi Kim," at a loss for words and surprised that two minutes went by so slowly. "Okay, well, bye. See you later."

Jessica touched Kim's hand gently. "It's me, Jessica. I'm just going to sit quietly with you a few minutes and visualize you healthy and happy. You're coming back to us, I know it." As she left, she informed the doctor, "He's vegetarian. I don't know what you feed him, but he wouldn't want any meat."

25. "Give your soul this nest"

Luke loaded another sound file, hit "reverse," and zoned out.
His breathing slowed and deepened and he sank into the mysterious,
often beautiful subterranean landscape of the soul and psyche.
Listening to reversals helped him relax. The harsh glare of reality
became diffused, sounds in the room distant, he lost track of time
and went someplace else in his mind. A part of humanity that was
lost resurfaced and speech reversals appeared—messages and
metaphors speaking of demons and angels and awesome energies
from .... from where? .... from a Mind that everyone shares?

> **Shock me. / Mask the slime. / I'm worried. / Aladdin
> source it, please, not Lucifer. / You must value it. /
> Eagle in the Garden. Whirl. / The planet has a beat. /
> Wire into your whirlwind.**

For a while he could forget seeing the girls' bodies in Sandy
Creek, their muddy faces and the catfish eating them, forget Elaina
being dead and the puzzling discrepancies in the accident report. He
let audio file after audio file run in reverse from beginning to end.
When one finished playing, he played another.

> **I walk this mess. / The wolf serves us. / Shake the
> makeup. Surface nerves. The wolf roams. / I've lost
> the rhythm. You're a loner. / Love you. / Sniff that. /
> Need a root cellar to mask the larva. / I've had
> enough of this night, the lower rhythm. / It must
> flower. / Unconditional service, I am listening.**

"Luke."
He jumped, startled. "Ari. I forgot you were coming."
"We're going to Elaina's funeral." She wore a simple black
dress, her face streaked from crying. "Your mom let me in." She

pulled up a chair and sat next to him. "You're not dressed."

He looked down: jeans, a white shirt unbuttoned, no undershirt, and bare feet. "Guess not. I just wanted to listen some more."

"To the Kenny interrogation?" she asked averting her eyes from his bare chest.

"No, I don't *ever* want to hear that loser again. I'm listening to stuff I recorded off the TV. *Everything* has reversals in it. It's a another reality behind the world we know."

"You're scaring me. You're not yourself."

"I'm not myself? Who am I anyway? Who are any of us?"

"Please—"

"I recorded one of those tabloid TV shows where a guy accused his girlfriend of sleeping around on him and said the baby wasn't his. She insisted she'd been faithful to him. They brought out the other guy in question and the two guys got in a fistfight. During the commercial I analyzed their speech reversals. I knew before they announced the results of the paternity test, which the guys took before the show, that the woman was telling the truth. If it's that easy to determine who's telling the truth, what's the point of talk shows and trials? Reversal analysis could save a bunch of time and effort."

"It might not be that easy. Some reversals are poetic. We can't take something that's poetic as literal. How do we know the difference?"

He sighed deeply. She took his hand and squeezed it.

"I convinced Elaina to stay with the group and she's dead," he said.

"She *chose* to stay."

"I talked her into it. If I just hadn't—"

"No. You're assuming that everything would be fine *if only* you let her go, but it might have led to something just as bad or worse. We might all be dead today if she stayed. We can't know for sure."

"That's easy for you to say—you don't feel responsible for someone's death."

She felt the energy drain out of her. Weak and shaky, she said dully, "I *do* feel guilty."

"About what?" he asked.

She felt trapped.

"Tell me," he said.

Could she trust him?

"Trust me."

When do you decide to trust someone? He showed her his vulnerable side, but what would he think of her if she told him her secret? Elaina would blurt out her feelings, whatever they were. Maybe she should try that, but she wasn't a blurter; she eased into it. She cleared her throat. "One night in Iran we had a devotional; that's a little like one of your church services, but we had them in private homes. It's against the law in Iran for Bahá'ís to meet for religious purposes."

"What's so bad about your religion that it's against the law?"

"Nothing, but the radical extremists don't allow any religion other than Islam."

"People can't stop believing a certain way because it's against the law."

"I know, so we worshiped in private. One night my aunt and my 16-year old cousin and some other Bahá'ís met at our house. We played music, prayed, had a spiritual discussion, and ate dessert, Baklava." She cleared her throat again. "My aunt and cousin walked home—and vanished on the way." She inhaled deeply to steady herself. "We think a neighbor told the authorities that we were having religious meetings. The neighbor used to visit with Mom and me. We exchanged recipes one day and I told her that a recipe she gave us would be great to serve at our devotionals. I was a little girl. I was just being friendly and I wanted to please our neighbor by liking her recipe, but she grew distant." Ari's chin quivered. "Bahá'ís are persecuted: arrested, shot, hanged, stabbed, set on fire," she said softly, her eyes dull with pain, hand resting across her throat.

"Did that happen to your aunt and cousin?"

117

Her eyes welled with tears. They sat in silence. He waited for her to continue.

"They were found a couple days later in a shed on the edge of town."

"Were they—" he couldn't finish.

"Dead," she whispered, "forced to drink molten lead."

Luke mouthed the word, "What?" but no sound came out.

She stroked her throat, swallowed hard, and realized with sudden clarity that the habit she had of rubbing her throat—and fiddling with her necklaces—must have been her unconscious mind telling people what happened. Her gestures indicated the place where the people she loved were hurt—their throats.

"Unbelievable," Luke said. He sat there quietly, trying to make sense of it.

She realized that she needed him to be shocked. He had to have an appropriate response, equal to the gravity of what she told him, to feel justified in telling him, to feel comforted.

She sighed, "I just feel totally vulnerable, and now with this speech reversal stuff, life has become—" she searched for a word, "so disorienting."

He took her hand and kissed the back of it gently. She felt a jolt of something like electricity pass through her body. She didn't know a kiss could cover so much territory. He slowly brushed her hair aside off her neck, stroked her skin softly. She pulled away. Her heart pounded. She felt hot, dizzy.

He led her toward the small couch in the corner of his room. She pulled her hand out of his, "I can't." She wanted desperately to cling to him as though he could anchor her safely in the present and keep her thoughts from venturing back in time. And now the unthinkable had happened, he kissed her and probably wanted to again. High moral standards were of utmost importance to her, but he caught her off guard.

Flustered, she made a lame excuse as to why they couldn't continue, "We shouldn't make out before a funeral."

"It's what Elaina would have wanted," he insisted playfully.
She smiled.

He asked, "Can we just listen to a few speech reversals before
we go? Here's something I recorded off a news show, an interview
with a couple who found each other again after having lost contact
years before. It's really beautiful; touching." He tapped "reverse"
and she sat down on the end of the couch.

> **Come with me. Life is big. / Feel the power. / Whirl
> with it. / Kiss. / Heal my face. This'll make it right. /
> Give your soul this nest**.

26. Poisoned!

Luke buttoned his shirt, put on shoes, and he and Ari drove over to pick up Jessica for Elaina's funeral, but now, sitting beside him in the car, Ari had new concerns. He knew her darkest secret—what happened to her aunt and cousin—and knew her deepest guilt, how she felt responsible for their deaths because she told a neighbor about their spiritual gatherings. This was the secret that plagued her through the years. She doubted that her speech reversals would ever deliver enough of a detailed message for The Insiders to understand completely what happened; instead, she told Luke straight out and had to trust him not to tell.

"Jessica's house is something else," Luke said as they drove up in his Lexus to a large Victorian house in the country. It was a rambling, multi-level home with a wrap-around verandah, turrets, bay windows, and gables from another era, not like the big cookie-cutter homes they build these days. It was a complicated house, creative, and unusual.

"It's so Jessica," Ari smiled, "different, a little out of place, but very classy and elegant."

Jessica met them on the porch, "We've got a few minutes before we need to go, let's sit on the verandah."

Luke told her, "Kim's last word before he lost consciousness was 'Nika.'"

Jessica looked puzzled, "Nika wouldn't be mixed up in this."

"Why not?" Ari asked. "Her pastor told her that speech reversals are the work of the devil."

"She wouldn't *kill* someone because they don't agree with her," Jessica stated, her sea-green eyes darker than usual and troubled.

Ari said, "She's *sure* that God is on her side. Maybe she feels she has God's permission to stop someone who believes differently from her."

"There were white flecks of paint in the groove on Kim's car," Luke said. "Nika drives a white car. Let's check it for dents, scratches, missing paint."

"I can save you the trouble," Jessica said. "I took my car in for an oil change and Nika had hers there for body work. She said she scraped a mailbox. I asked whose mailbox, and she got angry and didn't say. I think she's mad at me because I'm still involved with the group."

"She wants to keep us from doing this work," Ari said.

~~~

"We're here for Elaina Ramon," Jessica told a solemn man in a dark suit who met them at the front door of the funeral home.

"Ah, yes, I'm so sorry about your friend. This way, please." He led them up a wide, winding staircase to the second floor and past several chapels. Thick carpeting on the floor muted people's voices as they paid their respect. "Here she is," he said, gesturing into the room, "Please sign the guest book if you'd like."

The casket sat in a small chapel, which smelled of carnations. They approached tentatively, unsure of how they'd react.

"She looks peaceful," Ari remarked, "like she's sleeping. It's not as frightening as I thought it'd be; terribly sad, but not scary."

Luke looked and turned away quickly, shaken. Jessica whispered a prayer.

"We just saw her the other evening," Todd said on the verge of tears, "when we found Karen and Sarah's bodies. I'm trying to remember the last thing she said to us. She was having an anxiety attack. What were her last words?"

"Something about her face being numb, I think," Jessica ventured. "She didn't say much at all after she saw the bodies."

"She and I talked after that night," Luke said dully, "when she called and told me she was bringing me the flash drive. She said she had to give it to me in person and would meet me at the grocery store; she needed to pick up something for her mother."

"Simple conversations become so important, thinking back,

when we realize those were the last words someone ever spoke," Jessica said.

"That damn flash drive," Todd said. "Whatever was on it must have been pretty important for her to die bringing it to Luke."

A young woman with dark, pretty eyes came up to them and introduced herself as Elaina's mother. Jessica told her, "We're so sorry about what happened. We loved Elaina like a little sister."

Elaina's mother smiled. "She had that affect on people. Please come to the dinner downstairs after the service. There won't be a procession to the cemetery. Elaina is going to have a green burial. We'll wrap her in a quilt that has been in our family for generations and take her to a special cemetery in a woodland setting where we'll put her directly into the ground—no casket or box. She'll become part of nature."

"That's lovely," Jessica stated.

Elaina's mother added, "I read a book about a search dog that pointed to a tree when the dog and its handler were looking for a missing person. Turns out the body was buried a year earlier near the tree, decomposed, and was drawn up into the tree along with water and other nutrients."

Ari mused, if Karen and Sarah were left to decompose in the stream they would have become one with the water eventually and nourished nearby plants, watered people's livestock, or evaporated into the air to become rain. Recycled; everyone would be some day.

Todd joined them. "Look," he said and pointed to a circle of webbing and feathers that hung from the casket lid above Elaina. "That's a dream catcher. Some Native Americans hang them over their beds believing that the good dreams slip through the center and drift down the feather to the sleeper below. The bad dreams get tangled in the web and evaporate in the morning sun."

"I'm going to get whoever did this to her," Ari whispered fiercely, her eyes ablaze with tears as people filed in, kids and teachers from school, Bull, Elaina's aunt Inez and several people who might have been relatives. And then Pastor Ted and Nika arrived. Ari knew that Elaina was Catholic so Pastor Ted, being Southern Baptist, wasn't there in an official capacity. Maybe he came to support Nika, a member of his "flock." Nika glanced at Ari and then away quickly.

Todd shook his head sadly; The Insiders were falling apart, dead, hospitalized, grieving, and at odds with each other. Elaina escaped the conflict in the group that would have surely upset her. He looked at the dream catcher hanging above her and whispered, "Sweet dreams, Elaina."

~~~

At the funeral dinner, catered by the Catfish Cavern, Luke and Ari positioned themselves one on each side of Bull. Luke said, "We have a couple questions about the accident."

"I'm off duty. Call me on Monday," he said through a mouthful of potato salad.

"It won't take long," Ari said. "Kim and Elaina were sideswiped. Why didn't you put that in the accident report?"

Bull shook his head. "They were drag racing; simple as that."

"Could the other driver have tried to run them off the road?" Luke asked.

"No. I told you, they were racing, I put my lights on, they tried to get away; one car bumped the other and sped off."

"You didn't get a license number for the other car?" Ari asked.

"Look," Bull said, more firmly, "there wasn't any foul play. It was just a big mess. I'm sorry your friend died. Case closed."

~~~

Luke and Ari joined Todd and Jon by the buffet and to Ari's surprise Nika came over. Jon set his plate aside to pour himself a glass of punch.

"I cannot believe this happened," Nika commiserated. "I hope you aren't mad at me for dropping out of the group. I couldn't take it if you were mad on top of everything else, those scary reversals, the dead girls, and now losing Elaina."

"Excuse me," someone said. They turned to see a smiling

stranger wearing a chef's apron over polyester slacks and a satin shirt. "I'm Pierre Lejune, manager of the Catfish Cavern. I've wanted to meet you and extend my condolences regarding the loss of your friend."

Ari frowned, he wanted to meet us—*us* specifically—as though he knows who we are or what we're doing? Why did he want to meet us?

"I couldn't help overhearing you talking to Sheriff Buller," he said. "How's your other friend, Kim?"

"Still in the ICU," Ari told him, feeling that he was being intrusive.

"But he'll be all right?"

"We're not sure, yet," Ari stated, growing annoyed.

"Was there some confusion about the accident?" Pierre Lejune continued nonchalantly, as though trying to appear conversational rather than interrogatory.

Fishing for details? Ari wondered. How suspicious.

"Sheriff Buller has things handled," Luke told him, and Ari wondered if Luke sensed that something was off, too.

"Well, then," Pierre Lejune bowed, "I'm off to refill the dessert tray," and away he went.

Nika turned to Luke, "You don't suppose this whole tragedy—the car accident, Elaina's death—is related to your work with speech reversals, do you?"

"What connection could it possibly have?" Luke said defensively. It bothered him that she referred to it as *his* work when she'd been in on it in the beginning. She continued to distance herself from speech reversals.

"This stuff is so weird anything could happen," she said, "but I have to tell you—"

"*Ummm,*" Jon interrupted. "*Ohhhh.*"

"Everything okay?" Luke asked.

Jon burped. "Oh, excuse me, how rude," and then, "*Ahhh.*" He scrunched up his face, sniffed, and slid his half-empty plate onto the table. He grabbed his stomach and doubled over. "I don't feel very well. *Ahhhh, OHHHH.*" He stumbled into the table. Red punch splashed out of his glass and slowly crept across the white tablecloth toward the edge. Luke helped Jon to a chair; he moaned, "*Ooooh, my guts are on fire,*" and then collapsed.

~~~

As the ambulance carrying Jon sped out of the funeral home parking lot Bull turned to Luke and said, "Trouble follows you, doesn't it? Are the rest of you feeling okay?"

"I think so," Luke said, looking at the others for confirmation. They all nodded, okay.

"Then try the corn fritters," Bull said, "They're real tasty," and went to get some more.

"I don't like that guy," Ari said. "Something's off about him."

Todd agreed, "Yeah, he seems kind of indifferent, but he's right, none of us got sick and we all ate the same food, and besides, food poisoning doesn't happen that fast. Maybe Jon has a touch of the flu."

"He set his plate aside when he got some punch," Ari said, "about the time Nika came over. Where is she, by the way?"

"She left when Jon got sick," Todd said. "She looked scared. But she wouldn't have messed with his food."

Ari shook her head, bewildered. "The only thing I know for sure is we're not in very good shape any more. Nika deserted us, Kim's in the hospital, Elaina's dead, Jon is real sick for whatever reason. That's four down, four to go. We're dropping like flies."

Pierre Lejune scurried out of the kitchen, raised a tray of dessert for Luke to admire, and chirped, "Bread pudding? I won first prize in a baking contest with this recipe," and then whispered confidentially, "It's got a secret ingredient: bourbon sauce."

~~~

"You guys *again*?" Dr. Owen stated when Luke, Jessica, Todd, and Ari came up to the nurses' station outside the ICU. "We've got to stop meeting like this. By the way, your other friend, Kim, is

125

responding to stimuli and trying to talk, but so far they're just incomprehensible sounds. We're watching him very closely."

"Maybe he's coming back to us," Ari said hopefully, wishing desperately for that to be the case. "So what happened to Jon?"

"Poisoned," the doctor stated. "Barbados nuts. They grow in Florida and contain jatrophin, a poison that's usually lethal. He ate the seeds. We found them when we pumped out his stomach."

"When would he have eaten Barbados nuts?" Todd asked.

"Jatrophin takes 15 to 20 minutes to kick in, so he probably ate them at dinner. I hear the seeds are quite tasty. He might have sprinkled them on his food like a garnish."

"They wouldn't have poison at a buffet," Luke said, "and no one else got sick."

"Maybe he was singled out," Ari worried.

Dr. Owen shook his head, mystified, and studied Jon's chart while Ari quizzed the group regarding suspects: "Kenny? He already killed two people. What's one more?"

"He's in jail," Luke said, "and doesn't know anything about us."

"Rusty who skipped town so he won't be arrested for being an accomplice?" Jessica wondered. "But he doesn't know about us, either, and if he did, why poison just *one* of us?"

Luke stated, "I wonder if Elaina's death is related to Jon's poisoning?"

"How about that creepy caterer guy from Catfish Cavern?" Ari asked. "He said he wanted to meet us, like he knows about us."

"We did meet at Catfish Cavern to talk about speech reversals," Luke remembered. "I wonder if he overheard us."

"I didn't see him there, and besides, why would he want to *kill* us?" Todd asked; and then he attempted a bit of humor, "We paid the bill."

"Of course we did," Ari smiled. "What about Nika?"

Dr. Owen looked up from Jon's chart and sighed.

"Can we see him?" Jessica asked.

"No, he's extremely sick. His parents are the only ones who can see him."

"Could the poison have killed him?" Luke asked.

"It still might. He's not out of the woods, yet. And the way this particular poison scours a person's insides, I have a feeling he *wishes* he were dead."

~~~

"Who has access to Barbados nuts?" Jessica asked when the doctor left.

"Nika's dad is a salesman for a Florida-based computer company," Ari said.

"He wouldn't bring home poison, like a souvenir," Luke declared.

"The Catfish Cavern restaurant chain started in a town near the Everglades," Jessica said, "but caterers have to be very careful about what they serve."

"We need to talk to Nika," Luke said.

~~~

Luke and Ari intercepted Nika going into her house and Luke asked blatantly, "Was your car the other car involved in Kim and Elaina's accident?"

Nika glared at them indignantly, "You wieners, how *dare* you accuse me of murder."

Luke said quietly, "I didn't mean to imply that you—"

"You *did* mean to imply it."

"I'm desperate," he said miserably. "Just tell me where you were the night of the accident." She scowled at him and said nothing so he continued, "When I asked Kim where the flash drive was that they were bringing us and who did this to them, he said *your* name."

Nika mulled this over. "You asked him *two* questions. He answered your *first* question, not the second. He didn't have time to chat; he was about to go unconscious—be happy he said as much as he did." She fought back angry tears. "He told you who had the *flash drive*, you bozo, not who ran him off the road."

"*You* have it?" Luke asked hopefully. "Did you get it from Kim

127

at the accident?"

"No, I told you that I wasn't at the accident. Elaina gave it to me earlier to copy—she had stuff to do for her mom—but I was running late and didn't get it back to her before she and Kim left to meet you."

"Why didn't you tell us you had it?" Luke asked.

"I was going to tell you at the funeral dinner, but Jon got sick."

"Why didn't you tell us *before* the funeral? There was time."

"I wasn't thinking clearly, okay? Give me a break. Elaina was my best friend. Here's the stupid flash drive." She took it out of her purse and thrust it at him. "Elaina wrapped a note around it." He took it from her and unfolded the note:

Bud Miller Real Estate; nude: exposed/guilty?
Zoo: a collection or a group (us, The Insiders?)

"Bud Miller is a Realtor," Nika said, "and guess what property he's trying to sell; the haunted house where we had our first meeting."

27. "Curse those trips to Bud Miller"

Ari watched Luke search his computer for the Kenny interrogation. "I'm sure Kenny mentioned Bud Miller. *Ah*, here it is."

> Bull: "So if you were to buy drugs here in town ...." **Slow down. Here we go**.
>
> Kenny: "I wouldn't buy drugs here in town." **Curse those trips to Bud Miller**.
>
> Bull: "If you were going out to buy pot around here, where would you go?" **I know who he's headed to**.

"Kenny's speech reversal was **Bud Miller** and Bull responded in reverse, **I know who he's headed to**," Luke said, "suggesting that Bull received Kenny's communication intuitively."

"Or Bull elaborated on his *own* forward dialogue," Ari said, "maybe *Bull* knows where people go to buy drugs."

"Maybe Bud Miller isn't a *person* from whom Kenny buys drugs, but rather a *place* where he buys them," Luke said. "Let's listen to what's on the flash drive that Elaina was bringing us."

> Luke: "So when do we get the reward?" **Say when**.

"That's *you*," Ari exclaimed, "when we went to the police station the day after we found the bodies and asked Bull about claiming the reward. Elaina recorded the conversation. Brilliant."

Bull: "It'll take a couple weeks to clear with the people who put up the money, Sarah's family." **Soon**.

Elaina: "Meanwhile, we'll call the newspapers with the story."

Bull: "No! Don't go to the media. It wouldn't look good."

Ari: "And what will you tell Sarah's family when they want to know who helped solve the case?" **Now let's discuss you**.

Bull: "I'll tell them that they don't need to know. It should be enough for them to know that we caught the creep." **Lucifer**.

Luke: "Make out the check to The Insiders.

Bull: "If people knew I used something like this ..." **a problem now, shake the beast** "... to solve a case, I'd be the laughing stock of the town." **Saturday's wolf howls in June**. "People would lose all faith in me."

Ari: "But it solved the murder. That's pretty impressive. If more people know about this technology, more people could be helped."

Bull: "We took so much flack for bringing in a psychic on one case we almost didn't survive that one." **I'm nude**. "People complained, religious fanatics denounced us as devil worshipers, and the former police chief lost his job." **Don't get me, Bud Miller**.

Elaina: "Did the psychic solve the case?"

Bull: "She gave us a decent lead, but no, she didn't solve the case."

Ari: "Well, this is different. Our work did solve the case."

Bull: "Just the same, don't discuss it with anyone." **My Lucifer flaws me. I see evil rotting**.

Ari: "But you could use speech reversals to solve other cases."

Bull: "Don't discuss this with anyone!" **They make war**. "Listen, maybe I could use you as consultants. You could be my secret weapon. I just don't want anyone to know how the case was solved, yet—not even my staff."

Bull: "I'm a little unnerved by all this." **I'll run your zoo into the ground**.

"It sounds like Bull has a reason for not wanting us to tell people that we helped him solve the case," Ari said.

"He's afraid Bud Miller is going to 'get' him; incriminate him? This is getting stranger and stranger. He mentioned Saturday in June. Should we check out the haunted house? This is Saturday and it is June."

"It might be another Saturday," Ari pointed out. "We're stretching it to think something might be happening *tonight*."

"But what if it is tonight and we miss it?"

She glanced at her watch. "Eight-thirty. It'd be scary going there after dark."

"We could take it real slow and at the first sign of trouble we'd be out of there."

"Let's go, then."

~~~

Todd tossed his backpack onto the front seat of his car and started home from the library. Ahead, on the side of the road, he noticed one of the empty squad cars that Bull used to deter speeders. It'd been in the same place for several days. Bull usually moved it every other day.

He pulled over in front of the police cruiser, walked back, and gasped. On the side facing away from the road was a huge scrape.

He peered into the front seat and saw the tip of a coyote tail poking out from under the seat on the passenger's side—the coyote tail that Bull usually hung from the antennae.

Was *this* the car—the *white* car—that sideswiped Kim and Elaina? Did Bull lie when he said they were racing another car that got away? If Bull's car was involved in the accident, how did Luke and Ari miss seeing the scrape at the accident scene? Because it was dark and that was the side facing away from them. Had Bull parked the car here, scraped side facing away from traffic, to hide it in plain sight until he figured out how to repair it without raising suspicion? Had the "weapon" that killed Elaina and injured Kim so severely been right under their noses all along?

Todd called Luke and Ari, and when they didn't answer, he left a frantic message: "Be careful of Bull! He might be dangerous."

Then he called their homes only to have their parents say that they were out for the evening and they didn't know where.

Jessica hadn't seen them, either. "I can't find them," he told her, "and they might be in serious trouble. Where are they?"

Then he called Nika.

28. The Crossing

The car hangs in mid-air, splinters from the crossing gate blizzard around it. Luke and Ari look at each other; something has gone out of his eyes like a light was turned off. Luke, to whom nothing bad ever happened, realizes the depths to which people can sink.

A memory blazes into Ari's mind, she touches Luke's arm, "The men by the corner of the house at the dogfights, passing a package between them, was one of them—" He finishes her sentence, "Bull?"

The car completes its graceful arc through the air, hits the ground with a jarring thud, sputters—out of gas—and rolls to a stop onto the shoulder of the road.

"Get out of the car, get out of the car!" Nika screams, looking back to see how long the train is that shields them from the men chasing them. It stretches as far as she can see.

They burst from the car and run as fast as they can down the dark two-lane country road.

"Split up," Luke says. "If we stay together it'll be easy for them to pick us off; at least one of us has to live to tell the story. Stay way off the road, but remember where it is so you can get back to it. Don't get lost in the hills."

The train rumbles on and between each car the ominous headlights of the waiting trucks on the other side—eager to catch up with them.

"Call 911," Nika exclaims.

"No, it'd go to the police station," Luke states. "Bull might be involved in this mess. Which way are you going so we can find you afterwards?"

"That way?" she says, pointing west.

"Great. Todd, which way are you going?"

"Home."

"Running *toward* those guys?"

"I'll stay up in the fields; they won't think to look for me coming toward them. It's counterintuitive."

"Ari?"

She implores him with her eyes, "With you?" but he shakes his head. "North, I guess," she says despondently.

"You'll be fine. Just stay away from the road. I'm going toward the Speedway."

"What if they have dogs and track us?" Ari worries.

"The end of the train is coming," Nika shrieks. "Run!"

They scatter in all directions.

Ari takes off across the dark fields, stumbles, falls. Rocks bite her hands and knees; blood trickles down her shins. She scrambles to her feet, hears a ghastly noise in the darkness; a rattlesnake! She veers to the left of the sound, prays there aren't more, and runs blindly deeper into the darkness. There are sure to be more snakes and certainly fire ants. Keep moving. If she can't see well in the dark, neither can the bad guys. A strange exhilaration spreads through her that surprises her.

She steps in soft earth up to her ankles: a huge mound of fire ants, but it'll take a couple seconds before they swarm to the surface and she'll be long gone. Keep going. Hot, dizzy, out of breath, she glances over her shoulder to see if the men are following her—no lights, no voices—and is stopped short suddenly and flung backward to the ground. Stunned, she lies there a couple feet from the barbed-wire fence that stopped her.

~~~

Luke heads toward the Lone Star Motor Speedway, a gigantic hulk of a structure on the horizon. On race weekends it's lit up like a ship on the ocean with a big sign that reads, "Welcome to No Limits, Texas." There's a gas station nearby; he'll call his parents from there and have them come and get him. Then he'll try to find the others.

~~~

Nika sits in the stock pond where she slipped and slid into the water. Great, just great, she says sarcastically and smacks the water hard with the palm of her hand. OMG, what if there are water moccasins in here? They're so aggressive they chase you. Exhausted, she lies back at the edge of the pond, too tired to care anymore. Going to take little nap right here in the mud.

In Sunday school they asked the teacher what kind of snake the serpent was in the Garden of Eden, and she said, "Only God, Adam, and Eve knew that," and then added, "It might have been a lizard at first, but God took its legs away to punish it for tempting Eve."

That sucks, destined to slither on your belly forever and ever— and all your kind forever after—but snakes are good at moving around on their bellies. They climb trees and swim; they make the best of the curse placed on them. That's admirable; but she didn't tell the teacher that.

A boy in her Sunday school class suggested that the snake was either genetically modified or a sock puppet—why else could it talk? The same kid questioned why God went to such great lengths to point out the *exact* tree—the Tree of Knowledge—that Adam and Eve *weren't* supposed to touch; like he wanted them to touch it. Couldn't God—being God—have put it somewhere else where they couldn't see it and be tempted? And then the kid insisted that Jonah couldn't have survived in the belly of a whale for three days— because of the stomach acid. That was the last straw. He was asked to leave the church and not come back. A few weeks later it was reported that he was seen going into a Unitarian Universalist Church.

Lying in the mud at the edge of the pond, with grit in her underwear, and a curious cow eying her, Nika snickers—a sock puppet—then bursts out laughing, and before she knows it, she can't stop—the stress from the last few weeks takes its toll—and she's laughing uncontrollably like people in the movies do when they're hysterical and have to be slapped back to their senses.

~~~

Being on the high school track team, Todd runs faster and

farther than the rest of them. He also credits participating in the "Warrior Dash" for the last three years, which helped to condition him. The "Warrior Dash" is a three-and-a-half mile obstacle course studded with obstacles from hell. People had to climb a steep cement slope almost straight up, scramble over cargo nets, climb a torrential waterfall, do the military crawl under barbed wire, run through a scrap yard of twisted, rusted metal, race through a maze, trudge through waist-deep water full of heavy floating logs, and finally jump over flames. It was fun, exhilarating, and done during the day, which didn't prepare him for stumbling around in a dark field with skunks and snakes and chiggers.

He runs parallel to the train tracks, climbs up the bank, sprints over the tracks, and slides down the other side. Then he notices that the armed men are gone. Apparently they didn't know that the car ran out of gas, figured the kids got away, so they turned around and left. If they'd been patient and waited for the train to pass, they would have realized their good luck and could have wiped out the rest of The Insiders.

~~~

When engineer John Paul called 911 from the train, Bull's deputy, Hank Cooper, went to investigate.

He finds Luke wandering disoriented on a deserted road out by the Lone Star Motor Speedway. When Hank pulls along side him, he starts to run, but he's easy to grab and take to the squad car. "You're okay, buddy, just get in the car and rest. The guy who called 911 said there are more of you out here. Do you have a cell phone?" When Luke doesn't answer, Hank hands him his, "Call 'em."

"No, if they see the police caller ID, they won't answer."

"Look, I'm on your side. Why do I even have to point that out? Which way did your friends go?"

"Nika went west."

"Good, that gives me something to go on." Using the time the call came in and where the kids were reported to have abandoned the car, Hank calculates about how far someone could have run west. He heads that way. It's easy to find Nika; all he has to do is follow the sound of her laughing, but she stops when she senses he's there. She stands up in the pond and throws rocks at him.

"Whoa, you've got quite an aim," he says, dodging the rocks. "Your friend's in the car."

"No, you're one of them."

"I don't know what you're talking about. I'm on your side."

She looks around, doesn't see anyone on the road, no trucks, no glaring headlights, no gunfire. She walks up to Hank and laughs, "The snake was a sock puppet."

He shakes his head, bewildered. Something weird happened to these kids. He leads her to the squad car, opens the back door, and she slides in next to Luke.

"Which way did the others go?" Hank asks Luke and he points north. Hank heads off into the fields and finds Ari, scraped and bloody, in a state of nervous exhaustion, sitting by a barbed-wire fence. He carries her to the car. She cuddles up to Luke and clasps Nika's hand.

Luke gently brushes the hair out of her eyes. "How are you?"

"I am going to so need a tetanus shot."

They didn't find Todd.

29. We Promised not to Tell

Hank rushes them to the police station and passes them handfuls of wet paper towels to wipe down their arms, legs, and faces. He hands Ari his comb. "Here, comb the dirt out of your hair."

They're all badly shaken, but between the three of them they piece together the story for Hank: the dogfights, Bull there, gambling going down and maybe drugs, Luke and Ari attacked by a dog, the car chase that could have killed them. Hank's jaw twitches. Luke continues, "We think Bull caused the accident that killed our friend and poisoned another. Bull was at the funeral dinner talking to us. He might have slipped poisonous seeds into Jon's potato salad."

Hank shakes his head "I almost believed your story until *that* allegation."

The door opens and Bull strides in, but upon seeing the kids, stops abruptly. Ari yells, "Get him, get him!"

"Ah, boss," Hank begins reluctantly, "these kids have a complaint." Bull glares at them and his nostrils flare. "I need to ask you some questions," Hank says.

Bull snorts. "Be careful, be very, *very* careful, you're about to cross a line you don't want to cross. You're putting your job—your career—in jeopardy. And you've got that pretty wife and those two precious little kids to feed." He looked at Luke, Nika, and Ari. "Get them out of here," he tells Hank and tries to dismiss them with a wave of his hand, but they don't budge.

"They have quite a story to tell," Hank persists.

"Yeah, yeah."

Hank steps close to Bull and says in a hushed tone, "I have probable cause to suspect you were involved in a felony, sir: dog fighting. Participating in the earnings and letting people use a particular property for the fights." Bull's jaw tightens and Hank continues, "I had Roger over at the Dalton precinct check out the abandoned house. There's evidence of illegal activity: blood and fur on the ground, trespassing on private property, bonfires unattended during a burn ban. If you're not going to answer my questions, sir, I'll have to take you into custody."

"Well, no bonus ham for you this year come Christmas," Bull scolds.

"This is serious, sir," Hank says, setting his smartphone for "record" and putting it on the desk. "Chief Buller, you have the right to remain silent. If you give up that right anything that you say can and will be used against you in a court of law."

"You mean anything I say forward *or backward* can be used against me," Bull quips.

Hank looks puzzled and continues, "You have the right to an attorney. If you cannot afford one, one will be provided for you before any questioning, should you wish one. You can decide at any time to exercise these rights and not answer any questions or make any statements. Do you understand the rights I just explained to you?"

"Yeah, yeah, yeah."

"Then please come with me, sir, *come with me.*"

Bull stands his ground, glares at Luke, and Hank produces a set of handcuffs.

"Don't mess with things you don't understand," Bull tells Hank. "Everything was fine until these kids came along. Spirit Mound was the perfect place to live and work and play and raise your kids. Now it's all coming apart." He scowls at Luke. "Tell Hank about the **ill water**."

"**Ill water**?" Luke asks.

"You know what I'm talking about," Bull snaps. He turns to Hank to explain, "You see, the water in the creek was ill because there were bodies in it; clean water wouldn't be sick." Hank looks blank. Bull grows agitated and orders Luke to tell Hank that Kenny's **wolf is sick**. "Tell him about that mind-reading machine of yours."

Luke reminds him, "You told us not to tell. We *promised* not to tell."

"Now I'm telling you differently."

Hank cuffs one of Bull's wrists and pulls his arm around behind him, then reaches for the other wrist. Bull is so intent on persuading Luke to tell that he hardly notices he's being cuffed. He demands that Luke "Tell Hank or he's going to think *I'm* crazy. And I'm not. *You're* the crazy one. You got me into this fix. Now you get me out."

"Handcuffs suit you," Luke tells him, "the perfect accessory for dogfight denim."

Bull turns to Hank and stammers, "These kids have a machine that they say can, *uhm,* play recordings backwards, *heh,* it sounds crazy, but this machine knows if people are lying."

As Hank leads him to a holding cell, Ari says, "If we don't tell the deputy what we know about speech reversals he won't know what Bull is talking about."

They consider this for a moment and then grin.

30. Snapping

Against the kids' vehement protests, Hank calls their parents and tells them to come to the police station and pick them up, and then goes into a back office to process Bull's paperwork.

When Ari and Nika return from the restroom Luke tells them, "I called Todd from the phone here at the station; he's fine. He made it to the golf course and called his parents from the guardhouse."

"We were *so* lucky you found us when you did, Nika," Ari states, blotting gently at her wounded arm with a paper towel. "You saved our lives."

"Luck had nothing to do with it," Nika declares. "It was Divine intervention. When Todd told me that he couldn't find you, I got the feeling that you might have gone to the haunted house. I had a copy of what was on Elaina's flash drive and I listened to it again: something about **Saturday's wolf howls in June** and **Bud Miller**, the guy who's trying to sell the house. I came to the conclusion that you might be there. It was worth a look, at least."

"So what do we do about Bull?" Luke wants to know. "It'll be our word against his and he'll lie. He has been good for Spirit Mound. People trust him."

"The blood and fur on the ground at the haunted house proves there were dogfights," Ari states.

"Coyotes killed something," Luke counters.

"Did coyotes make the bonfires?" she persists.

"Vagrants."

"What about all the footprints?"

"The footprints of everyone who wandered through the grounds last week—there hasn't been any rain to wash them away—and besides, footprints don't prove that Bull was involved."

Nika encourages him, "Regardless of whether people believe us, I think you should tell Bull what you think of him. In the meantime,

141

I'm going back to the washroom. I think I still have mud in my underwear."

"Ari, come with me to talk to Bull?" Luke asks. "It might do you good to see him behind bars where he can't hurt us any more."

~~~

Ari bursts through the door ahead of Luke, rushes to the jail cell, and accuses Bull, "You were at the dogfights."

He looks up from the cot where he's lying. "You're not supposed to be in here. Where's Hank?" He notices her torn clothes, disheveled hair, and bloody arm. "I hope that cut doesn't scar you. You're such a pretty little thing." He sighs and rolls over on the cot, his back to her.

She grips the bars, "Look at me! I won't be dismissed."

Luke leans against the wall observing.

Bull rolls over on his back and says more to himself than to them, "Have you seen Spirit Mound at twilight when the sky turns blue-black and lights come on along the shore of the lake like a string of bright pearls, and white herons fish in the shadows? It's enchanted. And the children," his voice breaks. "They're pure like those white herons," pausing, and then, "You have to get the big picture, make a few sacrifices, take some risks—to protect the children."

"The 'big picture'?" Luke asks. Bull doesn't answer, lost in thought.

"My daddy was a bull rider and my best friend, a rodeo protection athlete." He laughs remembering Dorky Dinky Do. He looks at Ari, and for a moment she sees something wistful and vulnerable in his eyes, like a little boy looking out. What changed him from then to now, she wonders, from a gentle little boy to an angry, controlling man?

He turns his gaze to the ceiling again. "My daddy lost his focus because I kept bugging him about something, and then he climbed up on top of the biggest, meanest bull—Twister—and Twister threw him real bad. He wasn't killed, but he was a broken man who never realized his dream of making a good living on the rodeo circuit and being able to provide for Mom and me. She and I moved to Spirit Mound; he didn't follow us. He couldn't settle down. He sent postcards occasionally, but then those stopped."

His eyes darken and his voice changes, develops a hard edge. "I was seven when Mom and I went to live with Grandma, a nasty, little old lady who resented us; she thought my daddy should take care of *her* in her old age; but there she was, having to take care of us. She was older than dirt and mean. There was something bad wrong with her, always cranky or fussing, looking to blame me for her unhappiness. And Mom got real strict with me so Grandma wouldn't get on *her* case if I misbehaved. When Grandma died I went to the funeral to make sure they buried her deep enough."

Ari purses her lips. Maybe guilt and loss changed Bull—that and Grandma's abuse and an overly strict mother. Bull tried to please everyone, but couldn't and kept getting angrier and angrier, and when he grew up, he took control. Everyone had to obey him from then on.

In some ways you and I are alike, Ari muses, each feeling responsible for other people dying or being seriously injured. She pushes her rising empathy for him aside and summons her grief over losing Elaina; she *will* make him confess. "Oh spare me the trip down memory lane and your sad story about rodeos and mean grandmas."

He ignores her. "*Yup,* I lost my daddy when I was just a little guy. Grief leaves a hole in your heart that never gets filled. And my best friend, Dorky, I never saw him again, he told me, '*Always* protect the people you love.'"

"You want to protect the children of Spirit Mound? *We're* the children—the *teenagers*—of Spirit Mound," Ari exclaims. "You'd crush us—the reality—to protect your vision of an ideal town."

"Where's Hank? Get him in here!" Bull orders.

"I don't know where he is," Luke says, "in the back somewhere, or maybe he stepped out for a minute."

Kathleen L. Hawkins

In the hall outside the jail cell, Hank, paperwork in hand, is about to go in and chase the kids back into the waiting room, but he pauses when he hears the curious exchange going on between them and Bull. He decides to listen.

Luke continues, "Life took your daddy and gave you Grandma instead. What a rotten deal."

"Yeah. I prayed my daddy would come and get me, but he didn't and I promised myself that I'd *never* leave anyone I loved, *no matter what I had to do.*"

"You were committed to the town," Luke says.

"Yes." Bull stands up and comes over to the bars to talk to him.

Luke suggests, "Maybe even a little obsessed?"

"You can't be a 'little' obsessed, that's contradictory," Bull corrects him. "I think about the safety of the town *continually.*"

"So at some point your grief about your dad and anger at Grandma turned into an obsessive need—I mean a *determination* to take charge."

"Yeah, do you want the likes of those men, those 'doggers' that you saw tonight doing business next door to you? I think *not.*"

"Dogfighting is quite a hobby."

"Hobby? Hell, it's an industry. A good pit bull with an impressive bloodline sells for as much as $10,000." He waits for Luke to be impressed, and then continues, "Thanks to me the doggers keep their business outside of town. I cleaned up Spirit Mound and I cleaned it good."

"You cleaned up the town and cleaned it good," Luke echoes. "But not all criminals are doggers. Some are burglars and some are bank robbers, but Spirit Mound doesn't have any of those, either; it's pretty much Paradise here."

"Doggers have friends. Word got out for them to leave Spirit Mound alone."

"Let me see if I've got this right," Luke says. "You know how the bad guys operate, and we're safer because of it."

Bull smiles.

Luke flatters him, "You're a trained professional who understands the criminal mind."

"You bet. You can appreciate that, can't you?"

"Yes, I actually can. You let them hold their fights outside of town in an unincorporated area—provided they don't bring their fun inside the city limits—in exchange for you looking the other way, right?"

Bull nods, pleased.

Ari's eyes narrow; Bull still hasn't confessed. She tells him, "What makes you good at your job also makes you dangerous. You understand the bad guys too well. You crossed a line and couldn't get back. You didn't beat the criminals, you joined them to get on their good side and gain their trust. That way you could tell them what to do."

Bull's aggravated that she jumped into the pleasant conversation he was having with Luke and growls, "Keep your friends close and your enemies closer."

"So you went to the dogfights and did a little gambling, and maybe some drugs, to prove you were one of them," she ventures.

The color drains from his face and his breathing grows shallow and slow.

Luke states, "You understood the bad guys, but Kenny wasn't a member of the criminal 'network.' He didn't know your rules or how to play by them. And to make things worse, we came along with a mind-reading machine and really screwed things up."

Bull's nostrils flare.

"It was useful to you that we read Kenny's mind; trouble was, we read *yours*, too," Luke says.

"I'm still trying to understand a few things," Ari says.

"Of course *you* wouldn't get it," Bull tells her.

"What do you mean, *I* wouldn't get it?" she challenges, stomach tightening, "Because I'm a girl, a teenager, or Persian?"

"You're a Muslim."

"I'm *not*. I'm a Bahá'í."

145

"*Whatever.*"

"So what is it I don't understand?"

"You don't understand Bull's reasoning," Luke explains, hoping Ari will realize he's playing Bull. "Well, I get it and it makes sense. How long has this been going on, the dogfights?"

"Some 10 years now, about as long as I've been sheriff."

"So everything ran smoothly—until speech reversals uncovered some secrets," Luke summarizes. "And, as long as The Insiders were the only ones who knew about it, you could nip it—nip *us*—in the bud. You could stop things before they got out of hand, before we went public. We're quite a threat to all your hard work."

"Maybe we *will* go public," Ari states.

"No one would believe you," Bull retorts.

"Yes, they will. All we have to do is let them hear Kenny's reversals when he says **I killed the girls, I stand. I give up**."

"A confession in reverse. No one will listen to you. You sound like crackpots."

"But you got his confession later when you questioned him about the **ill water**. You said he threw up and confessed."

"I recorded that? No, I don't think so," Bull taunts. "And I'm usually so good about doing things by the book, crossing every 't' and dotting every 'i' so the bad guys don't get away."

"We *saw* you at the dogfights," Ari reminds him.

"Oh, *pluheeeze*. I was there investigating."

"We saw you participating. Any one of the people there could verify our story."

He laughs. "Those guys aren't going to come forward and identify themselves. Did you get license plate numbers?" He sees the startled look on her face. "*Ha*, you just realized you could have done that. But then that would have been hard to do while you were running for your lives."

"So you knew they were chasing us, but didn't try to stop them," Ari stated.

"I heard about it afterwards."

"Officer Cooper found us wandering dazed in the fields."

"Because you were in shock from the amazement you felt for being so stupid trying to beat a train to the crossing gate."

"We were being chased by your low-life friends," Ari states.

"They're *not* my friends!" Bull erupts.

"Okay, your business partners," she says and steps right up to the bars of the cell. He's on the verge of snapping, if only she can bend him far enough.

"They're not my partners. I *hate* those people. I hate them almost as much as I hate you. Why don't you go bake some falafels or whatever it is you people eat? Just go away. I've got a man's admiration here," he says and looks to Luke for confirmation. Luke nods.

Darn, Bull's good, Ari thinks. Mentally she circles him looking for weaknesses. "Maybe Kenny knows the people who were there and he's got nothing to lose by telling. Are you and Kenny buddies?"

"No, what a loser."

"But you're acquaintances, right?"

"I am *not* accountable to *you,*" Bull growls. "Where's Hank? I swear he's going to get a reprimand."

"We saw gambling going on," Ari tells him. "How much did you make, on average, per weekend? I hear some guys can make $1,000 a fight."

"Are you kidding? That's pocket change."

"So it's more?"

He laughs again, and then to impress her, "Some guys make upwards of $5,000 a fight. A good night can gross $100,000."

She rewards him with a surprised look and it pleases him.

"Then there's hush money and a percent of the winnings," she says.

"Oh, shut up. Don't accuse me of being on the take."

She's almost grateful to him, now, for giving her an opportunity to reclaim her life. It's empowering to corner an adult like this. Sure, there are jail bars between them, but she has the truth on her side. Until now she'd felt like a victim, helpless to save her aunt, cousin, and Elaina, and attacked by a dog and chased by criminals. But she survived and has the upper hand. She's having an affect on Bull. He's just as caught up in the heat of her accusations as she's caught up in making them. She feels strong and centered.

Bull is losing his composure. He's all over the board; he likes Luke and hates her. He's defensive, angry, and racist.

"You bought drugs from those guys," she continues, her voice rising, playing on his anger.

"I did not."

"You *DID*."

"For the last time, you little snot, I didn't buy any drugs," he yells, stepping so close to the bars that they're now in each other's faces.

"All right, then, you *sold* them!" she yells.

"Damn right I sold 'em, you little b—" He straightens up, his face falls, he was caught in the momentum of her accusations; a snotty little teenager.

Still listening from his vantage point in the hall, Hank leans against the wall, disheartened. He used to have the greatest admiration for Bull.

"One thing led to another," Ari tells Bull. "You started by trying to protect a town, and then hung out with the bad guys to keep track of them, and then you saw how easy it was to make a buck. And, finally, you realized that if we helped you solve your cases we'd discover *your* secrets, too, and put an end to your lucrative, extracurricular activities. It was easier to pick us off, wasn't it, to engineer little accidents like the car crash that killed Elaina."

"I didn't cause that accident!" he scowls.

"You sideswiped them." She's pacing back and forth in front of the cell, "And that made them lose control of their car."

"How'd you know Elaina and Kim were going to meet us with the flash drive?" Luke asks.

"Surveillance," he answers. "I heard her talking to Kim and knew she was bringing you a flash drive with incriminating evidence."

"Why'd you spy on Elaina and not the rest of us?" Luke asks.

Bull looks at him with a sly grin. "Did I say I just listened to her?"

"You listened to *all* our conversations?" Luke says, stunned.

"How'd you place a bug in our phones?" Ari asks. "You never came into our houses."

"So naive. You don't need to go *into* someone's house to intercept communication these days. Wiretaps are so passé." He smiles, proud of himself, puffs out his chest, "Cellphone, smartphone, landline, text—has a nice rhythm to it, doesn't it, cellphone, smartphone, landline, text—whatever you got, I got a way to get it."

Luke pushes down his fear at being spied on. "That was clever, covering all the bases."

"Yeah, it's not like I have anything else to do, there's no crime in Spirit Mound. Listening to you all was quite entertaining."

"Kim and Elaina weren't drag racing, were they?" Ari asks.

"Oh shut up about that."

"There were only two cars, weren't there, Kim's and yours," she continues, "and you invented the story about a second car racing them."

"Yeah, so what?"

"How'd you get Kim to run from you?" she wonders. "He would have stopped for the police."

"I didn't use the lights. I came up behind him, caught him off guard, and rode his bumper. I just wanted to scare him so when I threw on my lights he'd be intimidated and wouldn't mess with me. I'd ticket him for speeding, find the flash drive, and confiscate it. But he freaked out and started to speed, so I chased him. I was really pissed."

"Then you sideswiped him," she says.

"Things got out of hand. Once I saw how scared he was, chasing him was fun, but I didn't expect him to lose control of the car and hit a damn silo."

"And Jon poisoned at the funeral dinner—" she says, shaking her head sadly.

"I didn't poison anyone," Bull says so evenly that she almost believes him, but then he adds, "Whoever did should have poisoned *you* first."

Luke comments, "That was inspired. Apparently Barbados nuts taste good. They could have been tossed onto his salad while he was pouring himself something to drink."

"Would you have poisoned us all, if you had the chance?" Ari asks.

"I *didn't* poison him, but it was useful; it put him out of commission."

"He got sick too fast," Ari says, "before you—or whoever it was—had a chance to put any on *our* food."

"What did you plan for the rest of us?" Luke asks.

"I hoped the dog would get you and that exotic little girlfriend of yours, but your friends came along. The guys in the trucks just wanted to talk with you, but *nooo*, you had to run and break through the crossing gate. Now *that* was stupid. You could have gotten yourselves killed."

Ari snorts sarcastically, "As if you cared about us being hit by a train."

"It would have been convenient," Bull admits.

"You'd kill all of us to protect the town," Luke says sadly.

"Not kill, just distract you" Bull corrects crossly.

"Distract us to protect your hush money, drug money, gambling money. You'd mess us all up," he pauses, to add effect to the reversal he's about to feed Bull, the reversal that alerted the group to Bull's hidden agenda, "You'd even **run our zoo into the ground**." Bull cocks his head to one side as if he recognizes it as his. Luke says, "Sorry, you don't have my admiration, and I doubt you'll get any from anyone else, either, once they hear this." He pulls out his iPhone.

Bull's eyelid twitches. "That's the oldest trick in the book; a hidden recorder. I've used it dozens of times."

"Because it works, I guess," Ari says simply. "And you fell for it."

Bull hurls a final insult at them. "You sure you remembered to press 'record'?"

"I'm sure," Luke says, "and I don't think I'll have to reverse *this* to get the information I need. It's pretty straight forward."

31. "Come and get me"

Dr. Owen shakes his head as Ari's mother approaches the Emergency Room desk with her in tow. He smiles at Ari, "You again; how are you going to make my life interesting this time?"

Maryam orders Ari, "Show the doctor your arm."

She holds up her swollen, bloody forearm for him to see and he winces, "Oh, ouch."

"Now tell the doctor what you were doing. Tell him how you got that gash on your arm!"

"I ran into barbed-wire," Ari says sheepishly.

"*At night* in the *dark* in the middle of *nowhere!*" Maryam emphasizes. "And *then* what happened?"

"Well—"

"The *police* picked her up; that's what. I had to go to the police station to get her."

"Mom, I'm okay. I think you're overreacting."

"Overreacting, *overreacting?*" Her eyes blaze with furious tears and Ari realizes that her mom must have been terrified for her, especially since her sister and niece were murdered in Iran.

"Let's step into the examining room and have a look," Dr. Owen says. He checks her over, "Fire ant bites, but no sign of anaphylactic shock, that's good, your breathing's normal." He cleans and bandages the wound and asks the nurse to prepare a tetanus shot. She comes back and hands him a needle full of something.

Ari winces, "Oh, *ow, ow!*"

"Is that a preemptive '*ow*'? I haven't touched you, yet," Dr. Owen says, needle poised in the air. "You're going to feel a pinch; okay, *now* you can object."

"*OW.*"

"Did that hurt, seriously?" he asks.

"No, but it *could* have."

He smiles. "Your arm might be a little stiff and tender for a few days; you can relieve that by moving it around."

"Can she vacuum?" Maryam asks hopefully and Ari rolls her eyes.

"Yes, if the cut on her arm doesn't bother her too much; she didn't need stitches so she should be okay. And get her a tetanus booster shot every 10 years, especially since she runs around with accident-prone friends."

"How are Jon and Kim?" Ari asks.

"Jon went home and is expected to make a full recovery and Kim's doing better. His eyes are open, he can sit up in a wheelchair, and his mood seems to be pretty good, all things considered, but his verbal ability hasn't returned, yet; at this point he's still incoherent."

"Thank you so much doctor," Maryam says and then, "Okay, young lady, you are going to tell me *everything* from the beginning, and don't tell me that you were doing a school project. What kind of project has you stumbling around in the dark alone by yourself and getting hauled in by the police? I get the feeling you're about to be grounded. No TV, no going out with friends, no computer, no Internet for a week."

Ari follows her out the door and calls back over her shoulder to Dr. Owen, "This is going to hurt a lot more than running into barbed-wire."

~~~

"My mom grilled the daylights out of me when we got home from the emergency room," Ari tells Todd, Jessica, and Luke as they sip lemonade on the deck of Luke's lake house. "And I'm grounded for a week."

"So what are you doing here?" Luke asks.

"I went to the grocery store to get something for dinner," *wink, wink*, "Remind me to buy it on my way home."

"How much did you tell your mom?" Luke demands, concerned.

"I told her that you and I were taking a ride on your bike and saw something going on at the abandoned house. We went to check it out and discovered an illegal dogfight in progress. The bad guys chased us and Nika came to the rescue, but her car ran out of gas so we jumped out and ran into the hills."

"Did you tell her anything about speech reversals?"

"No. I told her some time ago that I was studying a voice-analysis technique for school, but she didn't connect that with what happened last night." She touches her bandaged arm. "She made me vacuum the whole house to keep my arm limber after the tetanus shot. She's such an opportunist."

"Well, I got my Harley back. It was a miracle those Johnny-Six-Packs didn't steal it. And Nika's dad drove her out to the railroad crossing with a can of gas so she got her car, too."

"But best of all, we got a confession from Bull," Ari exclaims. "He confessed to allowing the dogfights and selling drugs."

"Yeah, we made a *great* team," Luke says proudly. "I threw Bull off guard by flattering him while Ari circled and looked for vulnerabilities. I flattered him, she *flattened* him."

"Good cop, bad cop," Todd smiles with admiration. "The 'bad cop' is aggressive and works a suspect over psychologically, and then the 'good cop' steps in and is supportive and understanding, which increases the chances of the suspect cooperating with the 'good cop.' Of course both cops are working together to put the bad guy away."

"I liked being the bad cop. I'm just glad Luke didn't try to defend me when Bull was insulting me. That would have broken my momentum."

"You were on a roll," Luke smiles.

"And you had the good sense to let me do what I was good at: badger him."

"You were fun to watch. You played off his sexist, racist attitudes while I fed his ego. He didn't know if he was coming or going. He got all confused."

"You were a great actor, pretending that you admired him."

"I *did* in a way. It was amazing how clever he was, how he

could explain every bit of bad behavior. Everything he did made sense on some level—it was just immoral and illegal."

"He underestimated us. He thought we were a couple of stupid kids."

"It doesn't make much difference, though. Elaina is still dead. And we have to figure out who poisoned Jon."

"Yeah, but some good stuff happened," Ari points out quickly.

"We got the reward," Todd grins, "$1,429 a piece."

"And Kenny's going to trial for murdering Karen and Sarah," Ari adds. "They found Rusty and will go easy on him if he testifies against Kenny. Apparently he went back to the trailer, found Kenny gone, figured he went to the bar to find the girls, and followed him. The girls were in Kenny's car because theirs had a flat tire—Kenny punctured it. Rusty followed Kenny and the girls and tried to stop Kenny from killing them, but couldn't."

"Kenny's going to trial for sure, and Bull might be, too," Jessica says.

"Maybe they'll cut Bull a deal if he identifies the doggers," Ari speculates.

Todd shakes his head, "A sheriff with a twisted sense of love for a town," and whispers, "God protect us from the good intentions of crazy men."

~~~

They sit in the warm afternoon sun, friends forever. How could they not be? Only they knew what each of them feared, loved, and survived.

The sliding glass door opens and Luke's mother comes out. "Nika called to say 'hi.' I told her that you were out on the deck and asked if she wanted to talk to you. She said no, just tell them that she might stop by sometime."

Luke marvels, "She can't stay away."

"Maybe she just wants to come back to debate the religious implications of working with speech reversals," Jessica muses.

"Well, whatever her reason, I'm done with this," Luke states.

155

"I'd like to be friends with her again, but I don't care if I ever hear another speech reversal. I hate listening to killers."

Jessica considers this and offers an observation, "We listened to Kenny's thoughts, a bottom-feeder kind of guy and so we heard the thoughts of a bottom-feeder. We started with the worst assignment of all: analyzing a murderer. Did we expect to be uplifted?"

"Good point," Ari agrees. "Maybe if we listened to a saint instead of a sinner we'd hear something different."

"The idea that we can listen to a psychopath's thoughts is so creepy," Luke says. "I went a little crazy doing it. I got addicted to listening to speech reversals. I barely slept, ate very little." He coaches Ari, "That's your cue to say something reassuring. I say 'I went a little crazy,' and you say, 'Oh, no, you didn't, you were just tired, you just needed some rest.'"

She remembers how obsessed he was. "I think you went a little crazy, too."

"Give him a break," Todd says, "We all had good reason to be crazy and depressed," and then turning to Luke, "There's so much left to do."

Jessica agrees. "We *can't* abandon this work. There might be more uses for it."

Luke shakes his head, "No, I'm tired."

"I think *this* will change your mind," Todd says mysteriously. "I visited Kim in the hospital before I came over today. His parents were there, too. He can't speak clearly because of the brain injury. So what's the obvious thing to do?" He grins and holds up his iPhone. "I asked him how he was doing. He saw that I was recording him, looked straight at me, and mumbled something that didn't make any sense—but when I reversed it, it said **come and get me**."

They listen to it over and over, first forward, and then in reverse at different speeds. Todd states, "We were all there with him—me and his mom and dad—so for him to ask us to *come* and get him, when we were already there, wouldn't make sense; I think his speech reversal is more symbolic than literal." He plays the garbled forward speech first, then the reversal: **come and get me**. "He's trapped in a body that doesn't work right, yet. He needs someone to come and get him out of there, out of the jumbled speech, someone to interpret for him."

"Someone with a mind-reading machine," Ari says softly.

They sit quietly absorbing the impact of Kim's heart-wrenching words. Luke brightens. "Maybe there is something we can do to help people without jeopardizing our own safety, like help Kim communicate with his family—and us—until he can speak clearly again. Let's hear that again."

Come and get me

"Wait, there's something odd about the recording," Jessica says. "Play it again … *there*."

"That's just background noise, static," Luke says, "There isn't any forward speech."

"But I hear something in it, listen again," she urges.

No pressur …

"That's what Elaina used to say, 'No pressure.'"

"That's just your imagination. It's white noise," Luke says.

They sit lost in thought and then Jessica says, "I just had a wild idea. Have you heard of EVP voices, 'electronic voice phenomena'? Ghost hunters go to cemeteries and old buildings to record the ambient background noise, and claim that they can hear spirit voices speaking occasionally when they listen to the recording."

"That's crazy," Todd exclaims.

"Crazier than finding hidden messages in voices played backwards?" Jessica challenges.

Ari's heart leaps, "A chance to hear Elaina again."

"Isn't it worth a try?" Jessica asks.

"Do you think her spirit was in Kim's hospital room?" Ari asks.

Luke reminds her, "They experienced a tragic accident together. Maybe she's standing by him, even now."

Todd says, "Maybe we could record the background noise of places where we met when she was still alive, she might be there, too—"

"Not the haunted house!" Ari objects. "I'm never going back there again, and I don't want to go to the Catfish Cavern, either. That Pierre guy is creepy."

"We could record the background noise in the cemetery where Elaina is buried," Todd says. "That would be an interesting field trip."

Luke lowers his eyes to hide the hope he feels for hearing Elaina again, and the compassion he feels for Kim who, with four simple words, **come and get me**, pulled him from his anguish, and he whispers, "We're coming—for *both* of you."

The End

Meet the Author

Kathleen Hawkins lives in a small, north central Texas town. She's a professional speaker and the author of several books. She studied Reverse Speech™ for three years with David John Oates who discovered the phenomenon and developed the methods to study it.

Discussion Questions

1. Can you see a use in your own life for a "mind-reading machine" that tells if people are lying and reveals what they're thinking?

2. Would you want other people to be able to read your mind?

3. What if people's thoughts were made public? Should there be a legal right to the privacy of our own thoughts: all of the time, none of the time, or some of the time?

4. It has been said that houses symbolize consciousness. What might the "haunted" house represent in the story?

5. Who was your favorite character? How are you similar or different from him or her?

6. How did the characters grow or change?

   • Ari and Bull both experienced disturbing events growing up. How did they handle those events similarly and differently?

   • Do you think that previously sheltered Luke will be affected permanently by his experience forming The Insiders investigative group? How?

7. There were some loose ends in the story that leave the door open for a sequel.

   • What might happen with the "doggers" still on the loose?

   • Do you think The Insiders will hear from Elaina again?

www.ingramcontent.com/pod-product-compliance
Lightning Source LLC
Chambersburg PA
CBHW051827170626
46807CB00003B/1070